A
FINE
ROMANCE

by Cynthia Propper Seton

A
FINE
ROMANCE

a novel by
Cynthia Propper Seton

W · W · Norton & Company · Inc ·
New York

Library of Congress Cataloging in Publication Data
Seton, Cynthia Propper.
    A fine romance.
    I. Title.
PZ4.S4957Fi [PS3569.E8] 813'.5'4 75-40497
ISBN 0-393-08742-5

Published simultaneously in Canada
by George J. McLeod Limited, Toronto
Printed in the United States of America
1 2 3 4 5 6 7 8 9 0

For Jennifer

A
FINE
ROMANCE

One

Through Christmas week of 1973 there wasn't a single good portent. In regard to the comet Kohoutek, things were doubly alarming. Astronomers had begun by announcing it would be as bright as the moon with a trail half across the sky, but were now reduced to hoping that it might be visible to the naked eye. The British *Guardian* had an editorial which began, "When economists predict a boom the canny expect a slump, but when astronomers predict a comet even the canny expect a comet. Surely this bastion of reliability is not foundering? Not at a time like this?" However, all bastions of reliability were foundering. No economists were predicting a boom. The Arabs had put their first embargo on oil.

For those among the educated reading public who had understood for some time that the earth's supply of energy was finite and would soon give out there was cold comfort, for the rest no comfort. People were grounded mind and body. It would therefore seem all the more remarkable that on the twenty-third of December so many as twenty-five tourists had the intrepidity, the heart, to proceed to their posting point in Sicily, a country that had itself begun to run out of energy two thousand years previously. About a dozen of these were English-speaking. There was a woman from Baden-Baden and a couple from Paris, and the rest were from the Italian mainland, including five schoolteachers from Bergamo. They were all waiting under the marquee of the Hotel Grande della Palme, watching their luggage being stowed in the underbelly of a CIAT bus. It was a deadly, damp morning and to warm each other an observation was passed from stranger to stranger—in English and in French but not in German—that with the ban on Sunday driving, on top of flight cancellations, etc., theirs would probably be the only bus on the road in the whole of Sicily at the moment. Hugging themselves against the drizzle, they might be smiling the smile of those who regretted to the bottom of their hearts the benighted day they lost their minds and signed the CIAT chit.

"D'you know," said Gerard Winters, an American physician, to his grown son John, "Freud believed that if he could trace the implications of one dream—if it were actually possible to hear the whole dream in all its detail—he could draw from it an understanding of the entire personality and character of the person who dreamed it." Dr. Winters turned his head and his fine eyes settled on his wife, her face animated by the challenge of speaking in French, and their three little plump-cheeked daughters, all with their chins up, listening. "Your mother and the bus are what put me in mind of Freud," he explained.

The father had a firm policy, rarely breached, he thought, of treating his older children as though they were his peers, as though in conversation with them one could expect at least the minimum in civility and attention. He held on to this policy rather obstinately while watching their ears stop up and their eyes become vacant.

The son looked across to his mother with *his* fine, but doleful eyes, which were expressing acute regret at having agreed to join his family for a week in Sicily. He certainly was not listening to his father. Nonetheless, his father went on, "It is entirely satisfying to your mother to commit herself, to commit all of us to a bus for eight days because of the anomalous moral problem of travel. Travel is good for the reason that it instructs and improves, but it is bad since it uses the world's diminishing supply of energy, but, do you see, if you do it by bus it balances out because a bus has the merit of being entirely deficient in grace of any sort."

Dr. Winters was a scientist who didn't know he approached his wife diagrammatically to see how things were going, for and against. It was himself that he satisfied by the Freudian observation, and through his son's silence which greeted it, he ran his eye across the group that had gathered, and noted that they were roughly people like himself in their middle years, but a little scruffier, and disappointing.

"I think this is the wrong bus," said John. "I think this is a senior citizens' trip."

Their fellow travelers were surely making equally charitable assumptions. For instance, it can be taken as certain that humanity to a man does not want other people's children on its tourist bus. The father and son, who had stood back to keep their connection with the mother and three little girls hidden as long as possible, thought they could feel the winces glancing off their cheeks. When their guide asked them to board the bus, absolutely no courtesy was shown to the mother and children. The Europeans pushed to get on in a way that embarrassed the Americans for them and confirmed the prejudices of the queuing English. The Winters, all six, took their places at the end of the straggle. "Self-control is the sum of the law," Mrs. Winters was often heard to remark to her children at home. And so here there was no need. Dr. Winters watched his three bundled, eager daughters, still dumplings stuffed with confidence, three *citizens* whose fair turns at the window had been carefully calculated in advance, and he had a frightening shock of tenderness for the whole lot of them. He knew that Kitty made a magnificent mother. By bringing up the end of the line he might not have to sit with her.

The guide, however, who turned out to be a little waif of a girl with a single thick black plait falling down the right front of her jacket like a bell pull, announced "Eppy fell-milly, sitsa all-a togethaire!" and sent them into quarantine at the back.

The son John eyed the plait. "Reminds me of Eyeore's tail and I think I'll see if it is a tail," he said cheering up and thereupon did not follow his "eppy fellmilly" to the back. His father gave him a short, dour look and proceeded up the aisle. The two smallest Winters girls were sitting together, crayons and chewing-gum packages clutched in their fists, and behind them were their mother and Annie by the window, her map of Sicily sliding off her lap and her glasses off her nose.

"Take some time to yourself, Kitty. I'll stay with Annie. I've got a street map of Palermo we can follow together." Annie's moonface, all truth and hope, was turned up to watch for the decision. It looked like a smile button.

Her mother, not all truth, said, "Oh that's all right, Gerard. I want to sit with Annie," but was persuaded to go back by herself.

Father and daughter thereupon spread out the map on Annie's knees and tried to mark their progress, but the bus beetled too fast for their Italian because the streets were empty and Annie became diverted by the cats. The children had an awful ambivalence about the cats, Annie in particular. She could not get over the quantity of cats in Italy. In the Colosseum, without moving herself one inch, she counted thirty-eight bathing on the stone in the winter sunlight. They had to make her stop counting in the Forum.

"I was thinking when I was in Rome," said Annie, "that it was too bad they weren't in Boston."

"Come on, Annie," said her father. "We don't take cats that *belong* to people, you know that." (The implication was that they did.)

"Oh, I know you would never do such a thing, daddy. Only I always wondered that if you needed one cat a day for your research . . . you might run out. I don't see a lot of cats around Boston," she noted a little uneasily, and then said, "what a solution to do your experiments if you lived in Italy! That's what I thought at first. But now I've changed my mind. Do you want to know what I think now?"

"Mmm-hmmm," said the father in an encouraging little tune of *mm*s that went up and down.

"Well, now I think that the cats in Italy are like elephants in Africa or monkeys in a forest . . . and they have their own country. And it really would be worse for a scientist to take them because it would be like going into another country and making the people *slaves,*" said the child, quite charged with enthusiasm, "and *killing* them in order to perform their . . ."

"Good God, Annie, you're losing your sense of proportion." And the father restored her proportion.

They were bumping off into the hills now where, if there were any cats, they were prowling hidden in the mist. Annie relinquished the subject by whispering did her father ever see such a tall lady, catching her finger from pointing just in time. Her father, predictably, said sssh. They fell quiet.

Outside, the heavy sky pressed all the color from the hills. The bus strained slowly up and around the bends of the road and from time to time, when the passengers were the least defended against hearing it, its horn gave out a brassy bleat. Gerard Winters was bored by the monotony of hills, any hills, Maine hills, and closed his eyes. His wife came from Watertown, Maine.

Kitty Winters sat in the seat behind, by herself. She had come a long way from Watertown, Maine, where her father had been a lawyer and her mother played bridge. She wore blue stockings which were appropriate when it is known that the first women to be called blue stockings, gathering together in London in about 1750, had "exerted themselves to substitute for card playing . . . more intellectual modes of spending the time." In Boston about 1950 that is exactly what Kitty had exerted herself to do. She had since read her way through the bearing and rearing of six children, and had found it a quite satisfactory division of labor until she joined a woman's support group, casually, during cocktails the Christmas of '70, and was at this point the only woman of the original ten who had not left her family. Of course, she understood that it was a coincidence for things to fall out that way in her group. She was the oldest, forty-seven. And nobody else had six children. And her voice was always the conservative voice. Nonetheless, she as well as the others had pulled out from the past the whole successful, productive history of herself and broken it to pieces. Together they laughed at the parts with high moral purpose and they wept for the waste of wit and humor. There was a stretch of time when she thought seriously of leaving Gerard. She had entered the Harvard University graduate school in history the previous year.

Handsome, tidy, good legs in the blue stockings, mind-improving, she was curled against the bus window reading Braudel's *The Mediterranean and the Mediterranean World in the Age of Philip II*, volume 2, looking very like the Kitty of three years back, but she thought she was a different woman to the bone. The new, primary, and autonomous Kitty Winters had re-embraced her lot, after the considerable bitterness, anger, and outrage attendant upon re-examining the history of herself. She had passed through the only crisis of her life, and she was safely, she thought, on the other side, triumphant with self-respect. There were only a few loose ends, all of them connected to Gerard. Gerard had lived through these few years with the greatest patience toward her and the least possible understanding he could manage. Moreover, he did not know the crisis was over, did not know there had been a crisis.

About two hours along the bus pulled into a spanking new service area that had been dug out of a hill like a quarry and they could all go to the bathroom. The bathrooms were splendid. It was all splendid, with magnificent terrazzo floors two men were sweeping, with enormous chromium espresso machines two men were manning, with wide windows awhirl in spirals of blue Motta bakery boxes. There was a dining room where tables were set with white cloth and glasses and bottles of red wine, and one could smell cooking. However there were no customers whatsoever. Therefore it might have been expected of the numerous employees that they would smile a greeting upon this bus load, scant as it was. This they did not do.

Dr. Winters, not for the first time, wondered whether there really were cakes in the Motta boxes, and whether the dining room really would fill up ever again. He walked over to the bar, leaned on it with the heels of his hands, and selecting one of his ten known Italian words (*grosso*) bought himself a very large bottle of Chianti.

"Do you know what that bottle's called?" asked a fellow passenger at the bar, a large, ruddy man of about sixty with his raincoat and tweed jacket open, and the buttons of a tattersall shirt pulling over his stomach. "It's a *fiasco*. Italian for *flask*. English for this setup," by which he seemed to mean the handsome commissary. He took a second whiskey neat. Winters liked that sort of information and said he was curious to know whether the flop derived from the bottle or the bottle from the flop, but the other man shrugged the question.

"You're an American?" Winters asked.

"Born in Brussels of American parents, carry a U.S. passport. Lived in twenty-three countries."

"You don't find these shrouded hills a little monotonous?"

"No. That's not where I find my monotony."

This seemed curt but as Kitty had wandered over, Winters continued the conversation under the banner of civility. "When I read Darwin's *Voyage of the Beagle*," he said, "I remember being impressed by a certain tedium that seems to extend over great stretches of the earth . . . Patagonia, for instance. Have you ever been there?"

"Born on February 12, 1809" (pause) "Darwin."

"Is that so? Well, or take Tierra del Fuego, . . . all of it covered thickly with forest but only one kind of tree, a beech, he says, with leaves of a very dull color, and the constant rain . . ."

"Tell you an interesting thing," the other man broke in. "Once I was living for several months in the Ivory Coast in a rain forest which was so heavy there was almost no light and everything was a hard dark olive. Everything took the color of it; trees, earth . . . there were no birds, no birds at all . . . only monkeys. Well, do you know it was very compelling, that oneness of color. Finally I ordered all our Land Rovers to be repainted to match it."

"What color had they been?" asked Kitty Winters.

"Blue."

"Well," she said, made uncomfortable by his glance at her, which was more overlook than look, "it must have been an enormous job . . . I mean painting . . . all those Land Rovers."

"They were sprayed," the man said offhandedly.

"Now, you know, I find that interesting," said Dr. Winters rather warmly. "The evidence of an instinct man must have to step backward . . . to merge, . . . lose himself in the large scheme of things . . ."

"Well," said Kitty with an edge to her voice, "there's another sort of instinct that's a lot more useful—to take color on and to blossom and bloom so the bees can find you."

They were now all ordered, in English, French, German, and Italian, by the tiny Ina, the girl guide, little one-braid, to get back on the bus. Ina was a triumph in human programming. She had evidently been able to commit to memory twenty-five hundred years of statistical history in four languages to cover eight days. From time to time the eye of a passenger would brighten as he recognized a word from his own language. If she had said "In the year five hundred thousand before Christ, Syracuse was the largest city in the world with a population of 426," nobody would have been the wiser, take it all ways. Young John Winters remained in her proximity as if he were at the end of her rope. His little sisters circled round him and leaned against him. When he pulled out his package of American cigarettes, he would walk over to Ina and offer her one. She would take it with a smile and put it in a little tin she carried in her satchel. She now had five of his cigarettes. Dr. Winters noted this byplay in part with sympathy and in part with irritation. He was irritated by evidence of the incessant demands of lust.

"How childish!" Kitty said impatiently.

"Oh, that's what they are at twenty-three."

"No, I mean that fellow from the rain forest, the ex-tax-collector of Boggley-Wallah. A pasha with three horse-feathers!" Kitty did not like to be overlooked.

"Just a little bombast," said her husband carefully. "After all it must be quite a comedown, a tourist bus in Sicily after twenty-three countries."

"You're right, just bombast," she said, appeased.

Two

THE pasha with three horse-feathers was sitting next to his sister-in-law, S.-V. Hume, the writer. It was she who was the keel of their wobbly little family party of four, and he suffered from an apprehension that she might desert at any moment. Of this she was well aware. While they looked like cronies, these two, and had had an early history of special affinity, aging had estranged them. Their attitude toward each other as they went over the hill had turned quite warlike. But when they first met thirty years or so ago Cass—his name was Henri Cassagrande, but he was universally called Cass, even by his daughters—Cass and Virginia Hume discovered they had both been born on February 12, 1913, exactly 104 years after Charles Darwin and Abraham Lincoln. This trivial bit of coincidence, even among fairly sophisticated people, may be experienced conspiratorially as a sort of sign of election, and for this reason and others, in their early days, they were very thick. However, no longer. It was now December, 1973, and in the normal way of reckoning, Cass and Virginia ought to have been sixty. But one fine day she learned on her side of the Atlantic, that he'd knocked five years off his age, and inspired, she slapped five years on hers. When he heard, he took it as a slap at himself, of course, and was mad as hell. ". . . a defense against death that is both morbid and transparent," he had written, and steered clear of her thereafter. But he hadn't read her quite right. She took her five years with the intention of getting a march on old age, getting there first in order to be in a commanding position. It was altogether congruous to her nature to do this. Now the most untoward circumstances had brought them together again, and so there she was, sitting next to him, still a damn fine-looking woman, showing him up for an ass ten years her junior.

Virginia Hume was lean and had grown a little tubular, with a narrow face, and a pointed nose along which, by lifting her chin, she was used to taking her sights; but her mouth rested in an interesting and sensuous pout when not in use, and there was a mocking kind of humor around the eyes. People were drawn toward her, up to a point. She was vain of a fine appearance, and wore clothes that were both elegant and ecological: raw silk, unbleached wool, caftans dyed in spinach juice, amber beads, rings on every finger, and shawls and capes and scarfs woven in underdeveloped countries.

Sitting by the window of the CIAT bus, across the aisle from Dr. Winters, Miss Hume was taking every bit as dim a view of the heavily veiled hills as he. Events had rather bumped her along in the past week. She assigned the cause of her present predicament to the other members of her own party and particularly Cass. Cass had his head back and his eyes closed. Usually restless, uncontainable, he was abruptly and for the moment made docile by the "nervous breakdown" of his younger daughter Mimi. He was a man of heroic size, almost large enough to account genetically for Mimi, and he had thick, unruly, once-red hair, reminding Miss Hume of Poseidon. Disgusting, she thought. She suspected he was more than willing to pass for a fool, and was an object lesson; what becomes of a Hemingway hero when he doesn't have a *short* happy life. It would have amused her to learn that Mrs. Winters mistook him for the ex-tax-collector of Boggley Wallah.

The breaking down of his daughter Mimi from her towering height and her shoring up by a diverting trip through Sicily accounted for their presence on the bus. If one could account for this wildly inappropriate choice of action, and for her own participation, Miss Hume would have to begin with great, big, poor, touching Mimi. She sat directly in front of her aunt, her back as broad as a four-star general's, and she had stopped crying, finally stopped quivering. Each member of the family who had been called in to cope with her admitted a failure of nerve. Next to Mimi sat her sister, beautiful Alexia, one of the failures.

Mimi had been hitherto and appropriately the family pillar. She was indeed four star, distinguished from the others by a better character and a permanent residence. She worked for the Common Market Commission, living in Brussels with her ancient grandfather Cassagrande in a dark nineteenth-century row house earmarked for demolition by British property speculators intending to put up yet another glass office tower. Upon word of her breakdown,

Alexia had flown in from Washington, and later relating the story to her aunt, told her that her first thought, of course, was that Mimi must be hospitalized, that they must find a psychiatrist. But the grandfather was adamant. "Out of the question," he said. "A change of air will do the trick." He was unalterably opposed to alienists and their sanitoria.

An old satyr of nearly ninety, still piping the tune, buttoned and pinned into layers of clothing, he tottered over the Persian carpets and sucked at his gums and wheezed his words out, but, as Alexia said, "While he has trouble with his buttons, he doesn't with his marbles." When Cass, their own father, finally flew in from Geneva, a list of the best men in Brussels in his breast pocket, he was turned round at the door and sent off to the travel-agency people to find out about getting to Bombay for Christmas. But there wasn't a plane seat or a hotel room left in the whole of India. He came back, Alexia said, "looking for guidance."

Alexia lived in Watergateland and sometimes spoke the language. Older than Mimi by two years she was thirty-five, with remarkable reddish-gold hair, green eyes, and a smacking style, and her aunt had been exasperated by her since she was six months old. In regard to Mimi, Miss Hume had asked her with some impatience, "I don't understand why you didn't *insist* somebody be consulted?"

"Of *course* I suggested she might want to talk to someone . . . but she said she did not," Alexia answered after a pause, as if she first had to discard several other possible replies.

"It was hardly a question Mimi could reasonably be expected to weigh," said her aunt irritably.

"Well it seems not to have been a problem about repressed sexuality, Virginia. It was some sort of despair about the Common Market . . . its *agricultural* policy. A psychiatrist would be the last person to know anything about it. Of course, if we knew a farmer . . ."

It was uncanny, Miss Hume thought, the way they had all been immobilized for days by Mimi's situation. And in the meanwhile altogether diverted by these travel brochures, as though the booking of reservations *some*place was the first sound step to a cure. And all during this time poor Mimi, tears welling endlessly, was being coaxed by Alexia to take hot beef broth, to sit by the window, to wash her hair; obeying mechanically, only pleading not to be sent to a hospital, and submissive about the travel idea. It wasn't Cass, it was the old grandfather who discovered Sicily and the eight-day package which, he said, had the supreme advantage of having reservations open. Something to do with the weather, he had said airily. He was quite certain that they would be getting their fair allotment of heating oil, but that in any case the climate was milder than Brussels, one only had to look at a map. It wasn't the grippe, after all, that had taken Mimi, he pointed out. Furthermore, there were Mimi's archeological interests, which he himself shared, and he was only sorry, *Cass*, that he himself was not up to the trip. One understood that he would underwrite it. It was at this juncture when Cass suddenly also understood that he alone was to accompany Mimi, who was out of her mind in the bedroom, that he thought he would go out of his mind in the drawing room. Heretofore he had been the last word in inattentive fathers. Nobody was more poorly suited than he to restore a daughter to health, he would have assured anyone. His whole vast self heaved in panic and he called his sister-in-law Virginia Hume in New York. It was a measure of his desperation.

At the time of the call the apartment in which Virginia Hume lived was dank due to the mean-spirited zeal with which the building superintendent responded to the cost and shortage of heating oil. Her writer's cramp was aggravated by the cold. The university was in Christmas recess. She had been teaching creative writing for almost twenty years and was the queen bee of the department. Lately, it had become the object of unpleasant criticism. She herself was accused by some peers of having seen to the tenure and promotion of *weak* men and, by the proliferating feminists, of weak *men*. The feminists were taking the case to court. When Cass called, person to person, wheedling at twelve dollars per three minutes, she thought she saw a lot of advantages in getting out and taking charge while earning credit, and she said, "All right, I'll be right over." Arriving on the eve of the departure for Palermo, she said to herself that she had little choice but to join Cass and Mimi. Alexia made the decision to come at the eleventh hour, her prime time. And that is how she was accounting for their all being out of their minds in Sicily.

Cass now opened his eyes, tipped his shoulder toward Miss Hume, and said in a low, conspiratorial tone, "Fellow cross from me?"

"Yes?"

"Calls himself *Dr.* Winters. Thought it was a good thing to know. 'Course, he's American. Our luck if he's got his degree in hotel administration.

"Did you talk to him?"

"Bit. Probably all right. Reads Darwin."

"What was he like?"

"Hard to say. His wife . . . sort of good woman . . . reminds me of that awful Amelia Sedley in *Vanity Fair*."

"Not now, she wouldn't," said Miss Hume who had the entire Winters family easily under her surveillance. Cass shifted his bulk to look across the aisle in a manner he considered covert. The large fiasco of wine was being passed from husband forward to wife and Mrs. Winters with great aplomb and no trickling from the corners was carefully tilting it into her mouth. When she was finished she gave a swipe to the bottle top with her palm and passed it to the child by her side. That child, the biggest of the three little girls, did trickle. Meanwhile the two youngest had a bag of cookies, and as one of them reached round to share it she felt herself watched by the stranger who was Cassagrande. She smiled shyly and passed him the cookies instead. This was a little endearing even to a man who'd toughed it out in twenty-three countries. He took a cookie. Nobody was attending to the view through this and therefore, when the bus rounded another curve, Mimi startled them by a cry.

"Oh, look!" she called out from head and shoulders above them all, her voice throaty, her face awe-struck, and they turned at once to see what Mimi saw. The bus was rolling down into a valley. The mist had drawn back to the tops of the hills and there, settled high on a wide slope, was a Greek temple that had altogether taken the winter colors of the hills, lichen colors. It could have been missed. One might have driven by unwarned and not watching. The bus, however, pulled into its station and the twenty-five passengers, properly hushed and humbled, thinned

themselves out and disappeared from the minds of one another into this large, empty, silent bowl of earth. The only
sound was the light tinkling of goat bells. Thin white goats
and tiny yellow flowers were scattered widely in the scrub
and lost to view. The Winters children raced off ahead up
the slope and to the temple; the older people held back.

Miss Hume, though she had passed a spring on the Ionian
Sea, had not crossed inland at the time, and not having
crossed, believed she could not have missed too much.
Now, therefore, she found herself with her breath caught,
quite unexpectedly awe-struck by the Doric temple of
Segesta. When Mimi had cried out, she had stared into the
hillside and a moment passed before she realized it was there
at all. At one with its setting, elemental and lordly, Segesta
was a temple of a light dun stone, settled into the darker
dun of an infertile land. It was a sight of solemn uncommon grandeur. Miss Hume turned heady and she tingled.
She strayed off by herself.

In time, her tingle giving way once again to shiver, she
veered toward Mimi, picking her way carefully through the
knotty stubble. Mimi seemed as stolid as the temple itself
ironically. She was looking about her, standing tall with
her red tweed coat opened, her tricolored scarf of heavy
French silk untucked and billowy. She turned toward her
aunt with a beatific expression and said in a hushed voice,
"C'est prodigieux! C'est pharamineux!" Miss Hume smiled
and nodded with an understanding she did not have. Mimi's
French vocabulary was beyond her modest reach and she
had lost, it seems, her English. The most disconcerting
symptom of Mimi's mental disorder was her sudden inability
not only to speak English but to understand it. It was the

sort of symptom one doubted and set traps for. Miss Hume
was tempted to point out that Mimi had just said "Oh,
look," but forebore to do so. Instead, bobbing her head in
a manner she intended to be encouraging, she gave Mimi
a little wave and ambled up toward the temple to join Cass
and Alexia. Together, they congratulated themselves upon
the significant progress Mimi had already made by saying
"Oh, look."

By now all of the twenty-five passengers had made their
way up to the temple and were passing round its columns,
counting them, looking to the tops of them, trying to re-
kindle their first moments of unutterable wonder while having their teeth chatter. Virginia Hume, scanning for signs
of the call to retreat, watched Ina the girl guide bob from
one cluster of kindly tourists to another to deliver the story
of Segesta in what she took to be their language. To avoid
this instruction she slipped down for a crouching seat on
the stylobate behind one of the thirty-six columns. Before
her was the vast valley without a sign of human life. By
rolling her forehead against the unfluted column and squinting she was able to examine with one eye the topography
and the trade routes of the smaller indigenous insects from
the Carthaginian expeditions of the fifth century B.C. to
the present, probably brief, era of multinational corpora-
tions. There was nobody near her, but by some acoustical
trick she began to hear what had to be the doctor's voice.

". . . and when they began to build the columns in stone
they made them just as large and strong as they had in
wood . . ."

"They didn't catch on?" piped a child's high voice.

"No, not for centuries. In the beginning of history everything took an immense amount of time."

"They didn't have new ideas all the time the way I do!"

"Well, not with your confidence, probably. But, after all, Annie, here's the irony. Nothing seems to have lasted so long and so well as the Doric temples. When they did catch on, they built the slimmer Ionic columns and they must surely have been pleased to have made this logical architectural advance, but what they gained in grace they lost in sturdiness, as far as we are concerned, at any rate. Segesta isn't a ruin. Segesta is a temple."

"I might very well bring my own grandchildren back to see this temple and be absolutely certain it hadn't fallen down!"

"Very well, indeed!"

Miss Hume listened and thought they could probably depend on the doctor for their present purposes, if not his sanguine prognostications of a future.

Three

I'M certainly going to bring my grandchildren to Sicily," said Annie. "I've made up my mind. Earthquakes and volcanoes and ruins," she said with an enthusiasm great enough to topple even the stolid Doric, "they will love it. Any child would."

This child was strolling with her mother and father that first afternoon toward the flat and not very interesting site of Selinunte. Before them were the tumbled ruins of temples in gratifying giant heaps that could be climbed on top of and hid in and crawled through indefinitely. The two smaller girls were already doing it. They had been befriended by the tall Mlle Cassagrande. Annie, who spent a lot of her time crossing back and forth between childhood and the adult world, hung on to her father's hand as if to keep from running off.

Dr. Winters said, "Do you know what *Selinunte* means? It takes its name from wild parsley. This whole plain was once covered with wild parsley."

"That's really amazing," said Annie, her face turned up to her father appreciatively, her glasses glinting from the rays of a weak setting sun. "All of this parsley! That's an awful lot of parsley . . . a vegetable. It would be healthy," and catching sight of a sister on top of a pile of stone she said, "Do you mind if I run ahead?" He did not mind.

"How do you know that about parsley?" asked Kitty of her husband, coming up from her usual place two steps behind him. He would not let her walk side by side. He would lengthen his stride and she would fall back. She wondered whether he was aware of this. He wasn't.

"In the first place, it's in every guide book," said the husband to a wife whose policy it was not to consult guide books. "And in the second place, I was listening to Ina. At first I thought that Italian wasn't a very difficult language after all. I thought I was really beginning to understand it. But then I realized she was speaking English." He laughed at his own joke and Kitty laughed with him.

"I wonder if Annie will always remember this parsley," Kitty said after a moment, "because I have a memory about parsley. It was during the depression . . . I must have been very young . . ."

Gerard began to listen warily. There was something in her tone that warned him the story would score against him.

"I was with my mother at the butcher's . . . and she asked me whether I would like to do something very grown up . . . and she gave me two pennies. I was to go next door to the vegetable man and ask him for two cents' worth of curly parsley. Well, I noticed the two cents' worth made quite a fistful . . . and what I've remembered to this day is the sense of relief I had because parsley was a vegetable and therefore good for you—just the way Annie thought—and that people wouldn't go hungry after all because there was plenty and it was cheap. Of course, I never took it one step further and thought you'd have to be a goat to live on parsley. How appalling!"

"Jesus Christ, not for a child of six!"

"How insulated we've been since the day we were born —and still are," she said, insisting.

"We?" He did not like her habit of tarring him with her class guilt.

"Well, we've just been driving through the most stark impoverished villages . . . the people look so worn and hard and lined . . . everybody's in black, everybody's in mourning. I saw a terrible shriveled crone without any teeth. She looked a hundred, and I thought, my God, I bet she's younger than I am . . . well, that's what I mean. We're here to be intellectually satisfied, to be exalted by beautiful . . ."

"So we are," Gerard said mildly, backing out of the conversation. In all serious conversations with his wife he had lately formed the habit of taking small steps backward, out. He strode ahead or he backed out. He loved her, he was very proud of her, very respectful of her mind, her sensitivity, but there was nobody in the world more difficult to listen to. She always sounded accusatory, as if she thought everybody should stop fussing and eat the parsley. For her part, there was nobody Kitty found more difficult to talk to seriously and she was aware that her delivery was more self-conscious and mannered with him than with anybody else she knew.

They were now in the middle of what was once Selinunte.

Gerard Winters lengthened his stride and Kitty fell back.

Gerard Winters drew as much pleasure from travel as his wife, but he drew it in the wrong way. His visual, or perhaps aesthetic, sense was not as developed as it ought to have been. The sight of a row of columns against the white sky, all that was left standing of a mammoth temple to Hera, really satisfied him because his own eyes saw it, because this historic ground was literally under his own Boston feet; the stone his fingers touched had been knocked down by Hannibal's army in 409 B.C., albeit the wrong Hannibal, and finished off by an earthquake. He didn't receive his pleasure, he conquered it. He conquered it by amassing his data: how large was the army, how many temples there were and whose, how much parsley. Three years before, on the occasion of his fiftieth birthday, he decided he would go back to the beginning, to Homer, that he would start with the *Iliad* and read upward as time would permit, and he was reaping the rewards, here in Sicily, where he would cross the path of Odysseus and the Cyclops, and even take a sighting of Scylla and Charybdis. It gave him an immense pleasure, and it was more community-minded than scratching one's initials on a pyramid. Leaning against a giant monolith by himself now, with the temple of Hera against the horizon, the spirit of Odysseus, sacker of cities, entered him although he was a peaceful sort of man.

He was settled contentedly in his innocent and also instructive historical fantasy, surveying the stone, piling the statistics, when the pasha with three horse-feathers wandered into his foreground. The pasha was followed in another moment by S.-V. Hume, the writer, with whom

Winters had already had a friendly chat, and by a daughter, Mrs. Something-Something, a woman who was not only beautiful, but was the exact color of sensuality to the eyes of Dr. Winters. He watched with private excitement and a little guilt. The color of her was a tannish-red, a freckly pale reddish-gold, and the desirability of that color was imprinted in the technicolor matinees of his boyhood.

Winters was a man of restraint who respected the boundaries of his life. His sexual fantasies, in contrast to his historical fantasies, were a little morbid, a little sadistic, and a little frightening. His mind used barbed wire to restrain them. For instance, automatically he wrapped this woman in her tinted glasses, with her chic, her camel-colored jacket and trousers, in a thin netting of barbed wire, hardly noticeable. As to the morbidity, he acknowledged it, had lived with it a long time, and might have consulted someone professionally but was deterred by the idea of being cured.

"Benighted island, Sicily," said Cass in a greeting to Winters.

"I am Alexia Reed," said his daughter, unwound from the wire, and they shook hands.

"It takes some imagination," said Winters to them, redeploying that faculty in himself, "to see a city here large enough to require an army of a hundred thousand men to lay it waste."

Everybody agreed.

"Sicilians don't have to conjure anything up," said Cass. "Going to be driving through the area hit by the big quake of sixty-seven. Or Etna! Christ don't those people know life's a gamble! In the blood! Watch every puff of smoke, calculate the paths of boiling lava from every eruption, and gamble they won't be in the way next time. If they're lucky and survive, they eye that lava that's buried towns and farms, and as soon as it's cooled they carve it up for paving blocks and build themselves new towns on the self-same slopes."

"Ah, you've been here before?" Winters asked.

"Not since sixty-seven—after the Gibellina quake. We're a kind of jobber. Have us in, estimate the extent of damage, cost of rehabilitation, reconstruction."

"For insurance, you mean?"

"No, no. Relief people, Oxfam, World Bank, they ask us to look things over, make an assessment for them. But we're not necessarily jackals. Suppose they want to put in an industrial unit—hydroelectric, steel, fertilizer, in the heart of a jungle. We take a look, see whether it's a good idea, what sort of infrastructure would have to be set up, that sort of thing. I'm an economist by training."

"Hell, you're the last man one would expect to find on a tourist bus," Winters said affably but his tone curious.

"We're having a Christmas family reunion, actually," said Alexia Reed. "My sister lives in Brussels and we all met there and at the last minute we decided it would be fun to do a trip. I myself am devoted to our bus. It's the only place I've been warm since the oil embargo."

She was probably a damn cold woman, Winters thought. Her eyes were green, he saw, flecked with brown. The tip of her nose was red. She glowed with cold. In fact it was damn cold standing around.

They set off through the clearings and found Kitty among the rocks. Gerard did not say, "Shoo! Go back to the rocks." He put his arm around her for a moment to

insure her of inclusion and then they all resumed the obligations of the serious tourist to deduce the past from the
evidence at hand; in this instance difficult. Selinunte had
been a thriving port on a river long since silted up. It took
the disciplined effort of the addicted traveler to bring life
and meaning back to it. In the early dusk of a winter afternoon, across the great flat fields of what had been meadows
of parsley, was sprawled the rubble of what had been an
imposing acropolis. Winters, Cass, Virginia Hume, and
Alexia Reed were variously successful, one of them mum-
bling finally about being ready for the bus. Where could
it be? Miss Hume knew. She led the way, talking to the
Winters.

"I suspect a lot of people must envy Cass," she said. "I
envy him. Not the moving from place to place, but that
each place represents a problem, a discrete problem, and
when you've measured the dimensions of it, handed in your
report, you're quit with it. You've done what you've been
hired to do. And if the people of Gibellina are not properly
rehoused or fed or whatever it is, you're first of all not
morally responsible, and second of all you're off in a rain
jungle in the Ivory Coast, busy spraying your trucks olive
green . . ."

"Wrong, Virginia," Cass pronounced.

She ignored him and continued to Winters, "And so it
never builds, the questions never build . . . 'What in God's
name am I doing this for?' I suppose it's a question a doctor
isn't likely to ask himself. I mean with your grateful patients always right before you."

"You're a medical doctor, are you?" Cassagrande asked
brightly.

"Yes, but I . . ."

"Oh, fine. Good! *Excellent*, Virginia. Follow you through smoke and flame," said Cassagrande in a crescendo of feeling, his last words directed to Miss Hume, who had found them the bus.

Inside it was billowy with heat, the driver in his perch working away at his soccer pool, having evidently kept the engine idling through the hour.

"Not a Concerned Citizen, I guess," said Alexia with satisfaction.

They settled themselves, the first to return, Winters eager to continue their conversation, bring himself to the fore a bit.

"I don't actually practice medicine," he said, "because I am in research, cardiac research, and, of course, by the time somebody's sent along to me he isn't asking the larger philosophic questions with a lot of detachment."

"It comes to the mind of every man of sensibility, doctor," Cass said, "and I don't mean a hell of a lot of sensibility—it comes to his mind that he must—somewhere between the ages of thirty-five and sixty—that he must take his reckoning. Bound to be bad news. My line as well as the next fellow's. My sister-in-law is wrong. I do my best brooding on our fiasco in Sicily while spraying trucks in the African jungle. Fiasco, doctor, eh! Name of the game . . . Forty-five, fifty, what happens? Kind of romantic fatigue, exhaustion. I don't mean women."

"I'm surprised to hear it," said Miss Hume.

"Don't be silly, Virginia."

"Sex is the carrot and the stick, *I* think," said Alexia, who looked to Winters like a reasonable authority.

"I'm not talking about donkeys, Alexia," said her father. "What I'm talking about is a climacteric of the *mind*, not of the body. Now I think it's a kind of *appropriate* thing to happen, an appropriate depression, the onset coming at the first real flagging of zeal when one is especially vulnerable to the pointlessness of . . . oh, let us call it life in a post-teleological age. And like your heart diseases, doctor, one won't necessarily recover from it." He came to his gloomy conclusion with good cheer.

Winters, who at fifty-three was mildly aware of having jockeyed past two or three of those moments of truth, had been in fact negotiating another. He trimmed his response to Cass.

"A few years ago I read something that I found myself wrestling with," he began in a ruminative way. "I think it was Samuel Beckett . . . who said that the twin evils man had to endure were suffering and boredom. Boredom? Is that so? I thought. What an honor to bestow upon boredom. But then, after all, when you're bored enough I suppose you could call that suffering. And suffering seems to cover everything. So there you are, in a circle . . . meaningless . . . But, nonetheless, there was a time in my more anxious moments I saw myself . . . hanging on by my fingernails, and if I'd let go it would have been boredom I drowned in."

"Clinically speaking," said his wife clinically, "boredom is a sign of depression."

"I think I've got myself on top of it," Winters said firmly to the others, bypassing his wife.

"Ha-ha!" Cass cried out. "All you do, you see, is turn it upside down and you're home free. I would say that if you take boredom for your measure, that we live in the best of times, the least boring of times. Therein lies the antidote to depression. No meaning? No purpose, no progress? All chance? Heart sinks! Down you go! *But*," he said, wagging a finger in the air, "turn it all right side up. No purpose? All this," and his thick arm swept round to indicate the earth, "who these warriors and temple builders were in Selinunte, what you and I are now—all this with no directing hand, no *intention?* Amazing! Fascinating proposition."

Winters looked across the extent of the meaningless stone piles and felt amazed and fascinated, and Cass went on, "Stand on the shoulders of giants . . . Darwin . . . Taken a hundred years to realize Darwin. Once one sees it . . . once one sees the uniqueness of our situation, why, the great thing is that it doesn't matter whether it ends with a bang or a whimper, but that right now, before it's over, possibly *just* before it's over, one has a crack at catching on to the whole thing."

Cass mounted his argument with increasing enthusiasm and Winters was infected by the enthusiasm if not enlightened altogether by the meaning. He crossed his arms, rocked his frame from one side to the other in order to think through an answer, but was spared by the rackety arrival of his little children, followed by Cassagrande's tall other daughter. The children cried out with great surprise, as though of all people, and here of all places, they should run into their parents. Winters introduced them formally, Elizabeth, Anne, and Victoria, all queens. They were covered with the dust of centuries, barettes dangling by a hair, and shook hands and giggled and said, "How do you do?"

Their father gave a poke to the bridge of Annie's glasses and asked, "Well, what did you discover?"

"John," said Elizabeth, assuming a wry voice. Hat, mittens, everything in her pockets. She was always hot and they always bulged.

"He's given up on Ina. It's all over. He needs an older woman," said Annie, a student of TV situation comedies.

"Not one with braids. Braids are all right for children," Elizabeth added. She had two braids, both coming undone.

John reappeared and joined his family in a partial way. He took his seat beside Annie out of which he leaned across the aisle for a chat with Mrs. Reed all the way to Agrigento.

The children slept. Kitty dozed in a pretty way against her husband's side. The bus jogged and pieces of the hour's conversation dropped through the grating of Winters' mind, and he fondled them one by one. He was excited but not only by Alexia Reed. He set her, wrapped up in wire, with her carrot and her stick, on the shelf to be drawn out in time. Now he considered Cass, Miss Hume, Alexia, not so much for content as for style, the bounce. What he wouldn't have given for some anonymity . . . to take on these people unencumbered by wife and children, present a self that was unconstrained, uncorrected by them. Kitty would catch his infatuation, pull him down, ground him. John was already maddening with that awful bravado of American youth, putting himself on a first-name basis with the entire world, calling Mrs. Reed Alexia with that insistent, immediate intimacy that was so indelicate, so presumptuous. The bus bounced and Mrs. Reed kept sliding off her shelf.

Four

T HEY were put up for the night in the leading commer-
cial hotel in Agrigento. A general tattiness was the décor,
both the private and public rooms functional if the body
was tired but monotonous if the spirit was. There was a
meager minimum about the furnishings, not counting the
bathrooms, which were a rich maximum, newly installed,
and of a magnificent tile and mosaic, possibly reminiscent of
Byzantine seraglios to any who might remember them.
Miss Hume tested her bathroom but all its works wavered
in essentials, and she took to her bed. There she kept her
fingers curled in her armpits and her book on her knees,
deterred from resuming it by a lamp dim even in its heyday,
now no doubt further enfeebled by a meager flow of elec-
trical energy. A meager flow of energy might describe her
own private condition since little of it reached the ex-
tremities of her fingers or her toes. However, that other
extremity, her head, was humming with purpose; Mimi was
stabilizing; they must make use of the doctor, have him

prescribe a relaxing sort of drug, and then in casual conversation, not rushing the matter, they—Cass, Alexia, and she herself—would entice Mimi back into the English language.

It was at this moment that there was a knock at the door and a visit from Alexia who had swaddled herself in a bedspread of rose chenille, not actually unbecoming, and who held a bottle high in triumph.

"Irish whiskey!" said her aunt admiringly. "Where did you find it?"

"Winters, my new buddy."

"Good. We've got to cultivate him," Miss Hume said, prepared to push her plan forward.

"The son, not the father," Alexia corrected in the mildly amused manner with which she blunted this sharp-edged relative. "We went for a walk and we came to an outdoor market all strung about with Christmas lights. *That's* where all the electricity's gone. And we bought oranges and salami and cheese, really excellent goat cheese, and awful bread—now why aren't they good at bread, do you suppose? And then when we were in the wineshop I thought we ought to have the whiskey in case anybody got sick."

"That's why you weren't at dinner?"

"Yes. We had a picnic in one of those dark abandoned little sitting rooms downstairs. Not a soul comes by. My goodness, what a wholesome family they are, the kind you draw in kindergarten, a pyramid with a father at the top . . . positively archetypal. They've always lived in the same house in the same town in the worthiest sort of way. John's finishing medical school. Harvard. Harvard undergraduate. There are two other daughters, who declined to come on this trip, at Wellesley. Wellesley! I said, 'Don't you think of dropping out?' "

"The parents will be grateful to you for your fresh insights."

"In fact, Virginia, I'm very good for other people. *They* are *not* for me. There's the rub."

Miss Hume, warmed by the whiskey, loosened her blanket, and said dryly, "I hope you're very good for Mimi."

"Ah, Mimi," moaned Alexia softly, seeming to seesaw between anger and futility. "How to be good for Mimi? She's always been one of those people who are too fine for this world . . . like Little Eva or Little Nell . . . only she's Big Mimi, an anomaly. We're all anomalies."

"I am not an anomaly."

"She breaks my heart. I have the strongest maternal feelings for her. I've always had, when we were very little, long before mother died. Fortunately *somebody* had them for her. Do you know that when we were growing up I never even noticed what was happening to Mimi, that she was getting so much bigger than I was? I *still* think of her as . . . fitting into my arms better than I into hers."

Her aunt, who spied sentimentality under the bed of any expressed emotion, made no comment for a moment and then turned toward her own designs, elliptically: "I do believe she's feeling better. I've been watching her with those little Winters girls. She seems to enjoy them very much. I suppose she would have been very happy with a husband and children."

"Why is that? Nobody else is," said Alexia reasonably, and she fished out her glasses from underneath her rosy wrappings. They were as large as pilot goggles and she looked through them calmly at her aunt, the better to eat her.

"What about our little mother Winters?" asked Miss Hume, diverted and having first to repress her curiosity about Alexia's own marriage and then her annoyance at the glasses. "Don't you think she's satisfied? Kitty Winters? I think you can tell by the children's legs. They're sturdy. The mother of a child with skinny legs is a neurotic woman. You had skinny legs Alexia."

"Well, the doctor *looks* like a satisfying man. He has that easy, loose-jointed, grizzled, craggy Harvard way, talk about sturdy legs. His wife, of course, would be the one to say."

This sort of innuendo was distasteful to Miss Hume, stirring some latent anxieties in her, deriving from half-digested Freud, a gloomy fear that it was sexual energy that electrified the mind, that it was brain food, and she had run out of it. She rerouted the subject: "On the other hand, Mimi had the legs of a prize fighter. It certainly seemed as though . . . I must admit to a great shock when I heard it was *she* who had broken down."

Of course, Virginia Hume thought, there was no reason why either of them should be sane if there was anything at all in causation. One would have to say that their mother always looked very fey and, in the event, was what she looked. And then there was the constant removal from one fly-bitten provincial capital to another. Through it all one had to admire Cass for a certain double agility, for his always standing by, while at the same time, when he was needed you could never get hold of him, it was ages until you could track him down. After Mary-Agnes's death he had packed the girls off C.O.D. to his father in Brussels for a good lycée. They did not have a stable childhood, those girls.

"It's just possible," said Alexia, "that you can't tell everything by the legs."

Miss Hume rerouted the conversation again. "Little Kitty Winters," she offered (for sacrifice). "You know, I always think the man will be more interesting than the woman. I'm often disappointed. But I must say at first glance, Mrs. Winters looks like just the sort of wholesome homebody your father admires least. He's always been excited by an independent woman—a woman who is carefree, sophisticated, foot-loose . . . he wants *her* to stay home."

"I always think the woman is potentially more interesting than the man. I'm often disappointed," said Alexia. "As to my mother, she wasn't *care*free, you know." She spoke matter-of-factly. It was supposed that it was because her mother was *not* carefree that she walked into the Orinoco.

"No . . . but she wasn't wholesome, either," said Miss Hume with some family pride. It was her own sister.

"She was not wholesome by half," agreed strange Alexia, able to find amusement in this as in all conversation. "I have a theory about the profit in being wholesome . . . about sanity and insanity. Would you like to hear it? It's a little analogous to the story of the progress of medicine—that not until the third quarter of the nineteenth century if you were sick did your chance for recovery *improve* if you consulted a doctor. Well, it seems to me . . . that some time in the third quarter of the *twentieth* century your chances of making it, psychologically—of *not* breaking down—became better if you were half crazy yourself. It's a sort of adaptation. Darwin crossed with Camus. I mean an absurd world is tough on reasonable people."

Since she privately regarded herself as solid as the Rock of Gibraltar, Miss Hume did not see where she would shine in Alexia's theory and confined her response to an expression of skepticism.

"Well, take Mimi," said Alexia with just a suspicion of mockery in her voice. "Mimi's a perfect example. Mimi and the Common Market. They've broken her heart . . . I told you that. Only I was wrong about the agricultural part. I don't think it was the farmers. Possibly it was the *Arabs*, their not letting Holland have any oil. You know how Mimi is. Her life and her work are all balled up together. She's a rational, competent, humane sort of person who's devoted to the logic of uniting Europe. That's her whole thing. As far as *I'm* concerned, I don't give a damn about the Common Market. I don't even know what the hell they're selling. But it's Mimi's life, and she was justified in thinking when the crunch came they'd stand together, pool things out of *common* humanity, that they wouldn't scramble like rats. Actually, Virginia, Mimi broke on a very fine issue."

Alexia paused for a comment from her aunt which was not forthcoming, and then she added, "I see you don't think it's a good enough theory to account for a reasonable person's breaking?"

"A reasonable person would not forget the English language. A reasonable person would have stopped understanding French. It's the French who are the worst self-seekers."

Alexia left her aunt as she always left her, tweaked. Virginia did not, as a rule, like women and fortune did not give her too many to worry about; her late sister, and the two daughters of that sister, were her allotment. It is true she had been teaching mixed classes for nearly twenty years in her creative writing course, but she always expected more from the men, although, as she noted, she was often disappointed. As for Alexia, there was no question that she found her uncommon. Since common was a withering word for Virginia, who remained a sincere egalitarian by keeping her distance from the common man and flinching from his common touch, to call Alexia uncommon was to award the highest praise. Uncommon, beautiful, well placed, gifted in the manner of a Jane Austen heroine—she could draw beautifully, she could be an accomplished pianist, her needlework could win prizes—she refused in fact to stick to anything, and was as easily diverted as any of Jane Austen's heroines were. On all other counts, of course, they could not have been more different. Although Virginia did not approve of drifting at the age of thirty-five, or of what she thought was a lazy, careless dilettantism, or of what, she suspected, was a rather casual way with the marriage vows, Alexia's husband Toddy Reed seemed entirely unperturbed.

Five

THE answer to the problems of alienation, to the difficulties of building a sense of community, may be to put people on buses. By the second day these leery, mistrusting strangers were the oldest and best of friends and Sicily, over which they clipped along a single road from one archeological site to the next, was as intimately acknowledged as though they were overseeing their ancestral lands. As to yielding to the impulse of sharing the most private histories, hopes, misgivings, even love, with people who happen to be riding on your bus for a few days, it is another kind of instant intimacy. Gerard Winters had bridled at the insistence upon first-naming that his son and his son's generation seemed to take for the outer signs of an inner equality. It sounded to the father quite the contrary; reductive, mannered, shallow, like making your statement by not having your hair cut. In regard to hair, the doctor had patronized the same barbershop since he was a boy, as Alexia Reed might have suspected, and his grizzled head was mowed down at more or less regular intervals. In regard to the fantasy of timeless friendship on a tour bus, he lent himself to it with great pleasure. It did not excite his derision. It was not to him reductive, mannered, or even shallow.

Meanwhile the sometimes unacknowledged yearning that people have, whether they are traveling or not traveling, to discover in the man who is a doctor qualities that set him far above the commonalty to which they can willingly pay honor and, if necessary, tribute was a yearning that on this bus was wonderfully gratified. Just the cast of Winters' lean and lined New England face, the way he lifted his chin so that he could listen and see you properly through the bottom of his bifocals, answered this universal human need for a beloved physician. The thoughtful attention he gave to Ina's translation of Frau Fassbender's description of the pain in her right shoulder, his assurance that it was not her heart but a touch of bursitis, was confirmation of the wisdom of their choice. If she'd dropped dead the next day, she would have been criticized for misunderstanding the diagnosis. The retired colonel from Manchester, England, waylaid him in the Piazza Armerina and had him put an ear to his chest to hear his tachycardia, and he missed the mosaics. "How long have you been subject to these attacks?" the doctor had asked.

"Since 1945," said the colonel. "I was just wondering what you thought?"

"I think you've had the longest history of tachycardia I ever heard of," said Winters, who could take mosaics or leave them.

The doctor was *primus inter pares*, and the doctor's wife

was admired extravagantly, first for herself in not putting
on airs, and then for a mother. The initial alarm at the appearance of her children had given way to a proprietary
pride in them buswide, and Kitty was the beneficiary, a
madonna. Mme Bontemps, the wife of a French manufac-
turer of mirrors, wondered whether she wasn't of French
extraction, offered as a great compliment. The Roman
Signora Piazza suggested she might be Roman, meant as a
greater compliment. But Kitty demurred. Her people were
Yorkshiremen originally, she explained—that was where
she got her color. They had come over to Saskatchewan
as indentured servants, she said—Kitty was a great demo-
crat—and eventually migrated down east to Maine. Kitty
did have good, dark color and her hair was parted in the
middle and smoothed back, but she was a little strong-
jawed for the real madonna, her interests were firmly ter-
restial, and her recent shift to feminism tended to activate
the belligerent inclinations more than the reverential ones.
She was, however, critical of women's liberation; only, you
couldn't be critical of it.

In harmony with the warming up inside the bus was a
warming up outside. They had rumbled through a winter-
scape of dour, hard land, not even slowing through the
center of bleak towns where the blocks of plain blanched
buildings stood on bare earth, unrelieved by shops or potted
geraniums in the windows: not geraniums but black-and-
white mourning signs were the only decoration: MIO
PADRE, MIA MADRE. Now their route was roughly
toward the east, toward the balmier and more protected
land of orange groves and even sunshine and even an ap-

pearance of prosperity. Cass said the reality was that the fruit was bad and the rest of Europe wouldn't buy it, Common Market or no. Suggestions to improve the groves were resisted fiercely by the Sicilians. Sicilian fierceness was widely respected.

But whether or not it was illusory, the road to Syracuse was cheering and on top of that it was Christmas Eve. The air was cold but the fruit trees and palms were green, and the sky and the Ionian Sea were blue. Winters sat staring out of the window while the hills flattened to the sea and the groves gave place gradually to the sterile geometrical shapes of industrial plants, of refineries, pipes, storage tanks, and hundreds of chimneys whose bad smoke might mean good, hot water. The head of his youngest child was in his lap, the gall of his oldest on his mind. John, the son, spurned by the ridiculous Ina, and without the courtesy of a pause, had attached himself confidently to the sublime Alexia Reed.

Gerard, the father, was indignant. He had not, heretofore, found himself pitting his own manhood against anybody's and not, of all people, his son's. Indeed, he had spent nearly a quarter of a century of parenthood making way for his children, providing the broadest shoulders, spotting the highest vantage points, always sending them forward, always himself stepping back, and with no, of course, sense of sacrifice. Why wasn't he entitled to expect a little self-effacement now?

He brooded along these lines. He felt it was demeaning to see himself in this competitive light, and he shouldn't have been put there, but the young draw the line at thirty as a matter of political principle, and then they cross it at a whim. Marauders. They have a sexual energy that's always on horseback; there's a sort of indiscriminate galloping all over the place. They're insensible to *selection*, to the civilized, the more subtle interchanges between ripened minds that create, with time and timing, marvelous excitement, marvelous stimulation. Barbarians, they've got to prove they're alive every minute. Well, as Cass observed, everybody wants to do that.

They'd gone off together at the Piazza Armerina, he and Cass, to find the men's room, and some fellow they passed made Cass think of something that had happened to him last summer in Rome.

"Sitting at a table outside this particularly lousy café behind the Colosseum waiting for somebody, and I noticed that almost every fellow coming round the corner was giving a mindless pat to his genitals. Don't mean to suggest they were a league of rapists, don't you know. Don't think they were even thinking about sex. Just making sure they were alive."

And as they were following their bags up to the rooms of their hotel in Syracuse, John, who was not now sullen at all, was already bolting *down*stairs with a "See you later!"

His father snapped "Dinner's at seven thirty. Be there!" in a bullying tone he had never himself heard. Kitty gave a shudder. When the children were deposited, their parents settled themselves in silence into their own room—into a spare, spirit-dampening box of a room, Gerard with a familiar disagreeable sense that his conduct was under review. Was he forcing himself on the Cassagrandes? Was he ogling them? He felt Kitty's disfavor, his least pleasant sensation, and cast about for some normalizing remark.

"Another magnificent bathroom!" he said.

The bathroom appointments were indeed of such an advanced design as to leave one uncertain how to approach them, putting American plumbing to shame if one did not count that there would be no hot water until eight. If there had been hot water, Winters would have sunk in thought in it. Instead he fixed a whiskey and water for his wife, and put up his chin.

"It's amazing to me that you let somebody like Cass take you in so easily," she opened. She was on target.

"Hell, Kitty, I thought it would be all right to like him," said Gerard in a mildly bantering tone. "Seemed to me he had the credentials. He's crazy about Watergate, he won't eat American lettuce, he's *for* the miners and against Heath. Matter of fact, I thought he was damned interesting about the British situation."

"You mean that the labor trouble is evidence of conflicts unresolved since the general strike of 1926? That's hardly an original thought. Everybody thinks that." Kitty read everything and was informed beyond reason.

"It never occurred to *me* to think that," Gerard said simply and, as this might be too simple, added, "Virginia Hume didn't think that. Alexia didn't think that. And Mimi doesn't understand her mother tongue, if I may paraphrase Senator Ervin. I think that's damn queer."

"Oh, well, if it comes to that, they're all damn queer. I mean here it is Christmas Eve and why isn't Alexia home with her own children and her own husband?"

"Do you mean you gave her a good shake, but she still wouldn't tell you why?" Gerard asked with affection planted in his voice, and he ventured a little smile. This was his half of the peace offer.

"Actually it was Virginia who mentioned it," Kitty said, yielding half a smile back. "Virginia said—I thought pointedly—that it was difficult to pin Alexia down."

Gerard, looking thoughtfully into the distance, saw Alexia "pinned and wriggling on the wall," but he said, "Miss Hume—Virginia—you were talking to her. Does she strike you as being somewhat resistant to the Sicilian scene?"

"She's been here before. She's even lived here. They've *all* been here before and they all sound as though they're surprised to be here again. Well, after all, they weren't shaken up like dice in a box and rolled out in Sicily!" Kitty, now an ally, was laying out the Cassagrandes instead of her husband. She was uneasy in new places, with new people, and was always under a strain until they capitulated and liked her.

"Well, I suppose," he said, off the top of his head, "they're the sort of people who've lived everywhere, been all over the map. I suppose they run out of things to do . . . get a little punchy . . . *Mimi* . . ."

"Why do you always want to put down Mimi?" Kitty asked, restraining her annoyance. "She's really a very . . . stalwart sort of person . . . decent, dedicated, intelligent, and she knows a hell of a lot more about the Common Market than her father does. She works for it." Then her voice dropped and she stopped being angry at anybody for a moment, and with a confidential smile at Gerard she said, "Well, she loves our girls. Anybody who loves our girls can't be all bad. Really, Gerard, I think she's a very *kind* person."

"You think anybody who lets you talk French is kind," said Gerard, answering affectionately and with the intention of reinforcing the softer mood. But Kitty was no rat and did not reinforce readily.

"That Common Market," she said irritably. "I always had the greatest ambivalence about going in, do you remember?"

She was speaking for Great Britain, or as Great Britain, and Gerard who had no strong opinion on the matter said "Mmm-hmmm," a sound that was pleasant and encouraging to children. He thought Kitty regarded ambivalence as something imposed upon her from outside. She certainly had small tolerance for it. And as his own object was not now to save England but to restore Kitty's good humor, he hummed a little, he went off to use the bathroom, he returned to look out of the window and comment upon the crowds of Christmas shoppers and other homely things.

They had taken up their books and had been reading for a while when Gerard was inspired to ask casually, "You don't know where John went, do you?"

"I can only suppose he's trailing after Alexia."

"Do you think someone ought to rescue her?"

"She can tolerate a lot of admiration, I suspect. She's used to it."

"I don't know whether I can watch this kid on the make. I don't know whether my stomach can take it."

"It's not awfully attractive," she agreed.

"What I mean is I think it's a strange business . . . with

all his radical politics, his Roxbury clinic, the community health care service . . . that when it comes to women, he's nothing more than a . . . drugstore cowboy. Really it seems to be the worst sort of chauvinism. I wonder where he gets it from?"

"Do you?" she asked, and was immediately sorry. Gerard reacted with such lofty, overblown indignation it would be a day and a half before he got over it, and so it was she who paid once again, as she thought. It was her opinion that she had virtually stopped being prickly about his insensitivity, and nearly never took a poke at him any more. But he was indeed insensitive and he did not notice the reform in her behavior. He was mad as hell.

It was his opinion that no matter whatever else might be justly said against him, he could not be accused of disrespect for the belief that women were the equal of men. And as he had always had this belief, and acted upon it, he did not see why he must be subjected to endless discussions about the failure of other people to understand, and certainly not to taunts more properly directed elsewhere. From the moment he had decided to ask Kitty to be his wife, he adored her as his equal, he vowed to protect, defend, support this equal, and was solemn in his conviction that with this equal standing behind him he would be inspired and emboldened to dedicate himself to become a man worthy of her, and of his chosen profession. She did stand behind him and then he did all this.

But some time or other in the last couple of years she began to remember their wonderful hardships differently. For instance, there was a reference to their early days when they were young and had no money and he was a resident at the General and they were living with two babies in what was virtually a cold-water flat on Joy Street. He had been at the hospital night and day. "I don't see many of them working like that any more . . . the way we did . . ."

"Yes," she said. "We both worked very hard but you were fascinated by what you were doing, and I was often bored and lonely . . . often, often, often."

So that she had come into the habit of looking back on his lyrical quarter of a century as though the whole of it were laid with snares. She never thought he laid them, never accused him of that. But he knew she resented his not nit-picking at their life this way. But there was no profit in that for him. So from time to time, exasperated, she took a pot-shot. And so he bridled. This time he got up, put his rain-coat on, and said he would collect the girls and take them for a walk before dinner.

The children could not believe that it was Christmas Eve. Annie and Elizabeth, who were eleven and eight, were tak-ing the unusualness of things with aplomb, but Victoria, still groggy from napping in the bus, was very close to tears at the growing probability of no tree and no presents. Her sisters wrapped her up and told her sternly that she was a very lucky girl to be in Syracuse and she seemed to take hope. Downstairs the street was a lively scene with shops open and families stretched across the sidewalk strolling arm in arm. It was difficult to get past them.

"I think it's very interesting that these children wear red tights and blue tights just the way we do," said Annie. "They could be American children." She thought she would count the number of red tights and the number of

blue tights. Her father thought she would become a so-
ciologist.

They sauntered, window-shopping, up one side of a long
street and down the other and the city racket and above all
the smell of urban Europe restored to Gerard a feeling of
well-being. It was probably the smell of its pollution, a
private blend of motor oil and olive oil, he thought. It gave
him a great appetite. They were nearly back to the hotel
when they came upon a grocery store in the window of
which was a formidable-looking machine of the stoutest
steel with many wheels and gears. It was operated by a stout
and formidable-looking woman. It would have been a little
surprising if she had been pressing out auto parts but,
strangely, it was more surprising that she was pressing out
ravioli. From time to time the woman's eyes swept her
sidewalk audience with a look of the hardest indifference.
The Winters children filtered in toward the window to
stand completely rapt, but their father, behind them, was
a little disillusioned.

"It rather shatters one's confidence in the charms of
underdevelopment," said a cheerful voice behind his right
shoulder, the immediately recognizably throaty voice of
Alexia Reed. "I mean," she went on, and by the light of
the shop window Winters could see green paint on her
lids, which made her eyes look like turtles' eyes, beautiful
turtles' eyes, "one would have thought shaping pasta was
at least a cottage industry. Cutting out noodles by hand at
the hearth of your hovel, well, one conjures up the warmest
sort of images—foot rocking the cradle, toddlers with
running noses, that sort of thing. But sitting in this window,

before a heartless machine, with all that hostility hanging out, and on Christmas Eve . . ."

"She is a little weak on the spirit of the season," Winters said, laughing. He was enchanted by her not having John with her.

"Exactly. Somebody very happy should be doing this job on Christmas Eve."

"I *might* be happy doing that for a while," said Annie doubtfully. She had stepped back to join the conversation. "But I don't think I could stay interested, but if I had little hungry children that I had to buy food for and warm jackets and shoes I would still have to be home on Christmas Eve, unless we were on a trip—well, we wouldn't be on a trip—but every mother would want to be with her children on Christmas Eve."

"I'm a mother who's not with her children on Christmas Eve," said Alexia philosophically; but as Annie's face took on such a wince of embarrassed dismay, Alexia explained, "because they're with their grandfather. They're going skiing. They love to ski."

"Oh," Annie said with exaggerated warmth, "we don't have any grandfathers. They're *awfully* lucky." Annie had learned to balance her books at her mother's knee.

At dinner Gerard was full of Christmas cheer. It had not taken him a day and a half to recover his temper. Kitty, on the other hand, became moody when she was in the wrong, especially when she was in the wrong by mistake. It took her a day and a half to forget it. She thought this bus business was too kaleidoscopic for her, the sights were too chopped up, and she thought she was being undervalued by those other people—Cass and his family. She was in fact curious about S.-V. Hume, about befriending a writer, and annoyed not to have read any of her books. Why she had let herself be goaded by Cass, she couldn't say, no more than why she had goaded Gerard.

Six

THE Christmas-morning tour of the city of Syracuse was swift and comprehensive: two and a half calamitous millennia in two and a half hours. It was more than some had the character to take and when the bus let them loose at the Fountain of Arethusa, several passengers guarded the intention to stay loose.

A Winters child in a striped stocking hat said critically to Miss Hume, "It's funny to call it a fountain. You look down into it instead of up at it."

"I think you're absolutely right," Miss Hume said. "It seems more like a somewhat grubby grotto to me."

Whatever you called it, there was a small pool fed by a spring, filled with a great number of creatures—ducks, geese, large sea birds settled in their nests, and fish swimming in circles, and an abundant supply of garbage dumped in by the local citizens upon which they all fed. From the romantic myth of nymphs and gods one's mind was required to take quite a dive. The fountain was in the middle of a wide railed promontory on the water, all of it bathed in sunlight. Along the railing there were benches on which old widows and widowers sat, in black stockings and black serge, making holes in the pale sea, as if teeth had been pulled. Miss Hume spotted a free bench and said, "That's for me," and flew to it.

Mimi joined her. They watched the Winters family lined up by a street photographer, each of the daughters grinning broadly, holding a great red Poinsettia flower under her chin. They beamed at Mimi, wriggled their fingers at her, and Mimi beamed back, all rosy joy. She told her aunt they were enchanting, that they amused her strongly, that their mother was formidable, and her aunt murmured "Oui" self-consciously. She had tried to approach Cass and Alexia in the matter of being firm about English, but they had stared at her blankly. They kept her a little off center. When the picture-taking was finished and the Poinsettias returned to the photographer, the children came to Mimi to tell her it was time to get back to the bus and go to the stone quarries where the seven thousand Athenian prisoners had been thrown, and Mimi, smiling enigmatically through their English, got up and went. Her aunt called out, "En retard!" which was as close as she could get to "See you later," close enough for Mimi evidently. Miss Hume settled back into her place on the bench to welcome a sunful of vitamins beating into the top of her and shut her eyes.

The bus pulled out for the stone quarries and the square seemed emptied, but in fact other defectors remained in the shadow of the buildings. When Miss Hume opened her eyes for a few reconnoitering blinks, there all at once was Cass, crossing the promontory with Alexia and the Winters, husband and wife. Cass, catching sight of her among the widows, flapped his arms about, hailing her as the greatest find in the ancient world.

"My word," he boomed. "Just been talking about the dissolution of Western civilization and there you are!" (pause) "the great organizing principle!"

"Well, I believe women are *that*," said Kitty, smiling and looking rather striking in her navy blue as though, Miss Hume thought, she were quite high up in the Salvation Army. Kitty told her that she had had a good talk with Cass on the bus about demographic evidence for a population explosion in 1590. They had found this quite absorbing, and in fact he had persuaded her to leave the children to Mimi and skip the quarries so they could go on with it.

"Kitty's above all interested in the women's movement," Gerard offered in a tone that suggested he thought Kitty ought to have gone to the quarries.

"No, above all I'm interested in the Portuguese pepper trade," said his wife with a warning in her voice. "However, it's been done," she added with a sigh, and to Virginia Hume she explained that it was the question of a doctoral thesis, that there were tremendous things on women that have never been collated—civil records, church records, court archives.

"Dismal tale, all told, woman's" said Cass. "Lot often no better than draft animals. Seems to me it was some time early in your sixteenth century, Kitty—Turks were heading across the Bulgarian plain, commandeered all the oxen for their haulage." (Pause.) "Farmers hitched their wives to the plow." (Pause.) "Bulgarians."

"They don't seem more contented out of harness than in" (pause) "women," said Winters affably, enjoying his mot. He looked to Alexia for appreciation, but she was wrapped in a brown study, a blue scarf and a brown study.

"Ah," said Cass softly, "never want to undervalue women."

"I'm surprised to hear you say that," Miss Hume said with a reflexive irony.

"Most objectionable feature in my line of work—thrown exclusively upon the company of men. Weeks, months—middle of the jungle, reduced to conversation at the level of a dirty little boy. *Regression.* Like to *think* it was regression! What one misses, what one sometimes *craves*, is a woman's mind . . ."

"Ach!" said Miss Hume, and began to look about her for relief.

"Well," said Winters, "why don't we head off for the temple of Pallas Athena and praise her wisdom, and on the way perhaps we'll find something to get us in the spirit."

"Good, coffee," said Miss Hume.

"Not coffee," said Cass.

They strolled once more, with Alexia on a string drifting off to the side, across the promontory, across the sharp line between sunshine and the blue-gray world of cobblestones and commerce. No commerce this Christmas morning, but Winters, to his credit, found them a café, empty but nice. Its cavelike qualities, the usual dripping ceilings and so on, were plastered over with airline posters. Particularly, if un-

expectedly, was one exhorted to fly Air-India. They settled
down to the lifting up of spirits, although Kitty Winters'
spirits were already quite high.

"Have you come to Sicily because of a book?" she asked
Miss Hume, who watched her juggle her phrases to an
author whose works she had never read. "I mean I was
wondering what you were writing now?"

"Nothing! She's got the writer's palsy," said Cass.

"I've been working on a novel, Kitty, a comedy of manners. It's the form that I find most interesting . . . but it
may prove to be one more casualty of our several social
revolutions. Suddenly there aren't any manners." She gave
Cass the point of her nose.

"Trouble with her is she's got very high standards," said
Cass. "No sex and no psychiatrists. Very challenging!"

"You don't know what you're talking about," Miss Hume
said dismissively.

"Everybody in a vertical position! On your toes!" he
called out.

"One has to have a love affair. There isn't any choice,"
said Miss Hume, allowing her voice to express a certain
weariness she felt on the subject, Cass included. "They
won't publish a book without a bed in it. My grandfather
used to say if it doesn't have raisins, it's not apple pie. It's
sort of a bottom line, but, of course," she said to Kitty and
Gerard, as she had said to class after class of students, "the
love affair will be a metaphor for something else—an elemental shift, a springing free, a symbolic blunder. There's
an inherent plotlessness one has to contend with in the lives
of civilized people, you see. They don't commit murders, or

shriek, or have scenes. Their marriages, divorces, are muted, cerebral. It puts a heavy burden on love affairs, do you see? They're the only credible climax left."

"Actually, Virginia, they're not credible," said Alexia.

"Put your head back in the teapot, my dear," said her father.

"I may be naïve," Winters said, "but it seems to me that in Boston, among the people we know anyway . . . Kitty and I . . . everybody's got a psychiatrist, God knows, but if you discount the students, I don't think we have a lot of love affairs. I . . . don't . . . think so. Some great *quid pro quo* in the home of the Puritan Ethic, possibly."

"You are naïve," Kitty pronounced.

"The best men don't talk about their love affairs," said Cass.

"The best women do," Alexia said moodily.

"Alexia is melancholy," Cass declared solemnly.

"Nonsense! She's overslept. She hasn't waked up yet," said her aunt.

"You know, when they were burning witches in the sixteenth century," said Kitty, who was the farthest cry from being melancholy, "a few brave souls did protest, in vain, of course. They thought it was a theological error. They believed in the devil but not in his competence to make these compacts, and they wrote long tracts explaining that these old women were only *melancholy*."

"I myself don't think Alexia should be burnt. Not for oversleeping," said Cass.

"To be melancholy was to be quite mad," Kitty added.

Gerard pushed his chair back, giving his wife the round of his shoulder, which was a little rude to her, in order to focus the attention on Miss Hume, which Miss Hume did not mind. "Now, do I understand you to say, Miss Hume, that people have lost their manners and their sense of humor and so it has become difficult for you to write comedy?"

"They have lost their manners and Virginia has lost her sense of humor," said Cass grumpily.

The doctor now gave Cass short shrift, which was very winning of him, from Virginia's view. "The definition of manners I use with my students," she said, "is 'a person's habitual behavior or conduct with attention to its *moral* aspect.' I think of myself as a *moralist*."

"We all do, actually," said Cass.

"A nineteenth-century moralist," she said complacently. She felt herself now to be on home ground, relaxed, and immune to Cass, who was clearly silly, and engaged by the doctor, who was clearly intelligent. "It interests me to see how people of intelligence, decency, people of *character*— Addison said 'manners are what we in England call character'—it interests me to observe how people of character make their transactions today, in a world in which all the old supporting structures are buckling. To observe and record it. So that if one were writing about it one might want to bring together a number of rather ordinary, stable people who share the same sort of intellectual and moral values. *Not* severe neurotics, not alcoholics, you see, because theirs would represent other solutions, other . . ."

"I wonder you can find a quorum," said Alexia.

"You'd be surprised."

"I couldn't be in your book."

"You're not. Now among these *stable* people there is one,

let us say, who has come under the influence of a new idea so that his habitual behavior or conduct may alter slightly . . ."

"Damned exciting!" said Cass and thumped the table.

"It is exciting," said Kitty, rebuking Cass, although with a fond look. "It seems to me that it's perfectly designed for the feminist experience, Virginia, or have you done that?"

"There's nothing I like less than women's liberation," Virginia answered, too tartly but because of strong feelings on the subject.

"She likes Viet Nam much better," said Cass.

"Well, now you say you're a moralist," said the doctor. "Now just what do you mean by *moralist?*" He spoke with an easy adult authority of the kind that brings smart-talking schoolboys to order.

"I'll answer you with a story I tell my students," said Miss Hume, "a story about George Eliot. She was walking with a man by the name of Frederick Myers—a man who seems to have been some sort of religious mystic—and they were talking about God, immortality, and duty. The first, she said, was inconceivable, the second unbelievable, but the third nonetheless peremptory and absolute."

"I never heard that before," said Winters, rocking his arms in appreciation. "I must say that's succinct. Puts it very well. Those are the ground rules, you mean—for your characters?"

"Exactly," said Miss Hume with satisfaction.

"Oh, well," said Alexia, "if that's all, I think I might be in your book after all."

"Not on your life," said her aunt.

"Do you know," said Kitty shyly, "I've heard that story,

and there's more. Bertrand Russell is said to have remarked, 'Oh, yes, that was the time she was walking in the garden with Myers and she said there is no God and so we must be good, and he said, No. There is a God and so we need not be good.' "

"Excellent, my dear!" said Cass enthusiastically. "Think we can all get into Virginia's book!"

"Ah, everybody scrambling to get on board now, I see," said Miss Hume, her good humor altogether restored.

"With George Eliot, Bertrand Russell, and *you*, my dear, our sky pilot!" said Cass.

Seven

In time the party straggled up to the site of the ancient temple of Pallas Athena, where they had intended to worship. However, what was left of it were only a few fluted Doric columns which had long since helped to support the Christian edifice and were currently part of the wall of the cathedral of Santa Maria delle Colonne. The chanting of the Christmas service was now resounding through the stone. The cathedral rose from a sea of parked cars that lapped upon its very steps, and in order to make one's way, one had to pick through fenders, and Miss Hume tore her stocking and looked grim.

"I think," said Winters as they stood doubtfully at the closed doors, "their cult is able to outshout our cult."

"I wouldn't mind going in to hear theirs," said Kitty, extending the invitation with her smile. "I would be interested."

It was a measure of the different ways they tamed their

world that Kitty was eager to take a seat on a camp chair at the back of the cathedral and to merge herself with the indigenous people at prayer in order to stimulate her cultural senses. From Gerard's view it was an almost alien act, almost provocative. Really, the way to go about it would be his way—to have read the guide books, mapped out the territory, and so be prepared upon arrival to find the fluted columns, the remnants of the stylobate, the Norman font, the bronze lions, the mosaics, only wishing that the indigenous people at prayer would clear out so that he could see better. But on this occasion, when Cass said he would go inside with Kitty, Gerard thought he wouldn't, and without a blink of regret at missing the font, the lions, the mosaics, he joined Alexia and Miss Hume, who announced they could be found on those sunny benches by the sea.

They headed down the hill again, the two women and Gerard, he now quite free to cut his own figure, waiting for himself to do it. He thought Alexia had cheered up, or waked up. She did not have a mobile and expressive face as, for instance, Kitty had. The benches were empty, not a widow left.

"Of course," said Alexia, "they will have had to go to Mass. The tourist bureau would insist upon it. They are the picturesque part." She stood against the railing by a bench, her back to the water, and scanned the scene for widows. Her aunt sat down. Winters stood, foot propped, to make a triangle. He had a very good view of Alexia-by-the-sea.

"Look here, Alexia," said Miss Hume with a perceptible ruffle of her shoulders, "I want to tie a loose end. It seems to

me somewhat hypocritical of you—glass houses and so on
—to say that a love affair isn't credible. I'd like to know
what you mean."

"Only that it sounds awfully romantic. That's all," Alexia
answered in a voice musical with surprise, as though bewildered not to have been easily understood. "You know,
Cary Grant, crossing on the *Ile de France*—a little passé.
After all, Virginia, the only dramatic interest in a love affair
is that it's forbidden. One is asked to imagine stolen hours,
secret assignations, clandestine meetings, and a great deal of
emotional exhaustion. It requires a lot of time . . . for re-
nouncing, for longing, plotting, dreaming, for being doubt-
ful, for being guilty . . . But since today nothing is
forbidden, people do anything they please right off the bat.
They don't want to put in that time."

"It's just possible, Alexia," said her aunt, after a thoughtful pause, "that your appreciation of social behavior is not,
strictly speaking, widely understood."

"Not to mention character assassination," said Winters.
"It's unwarranted to believe Cary Grant ever considered
anything short of wedlock."

Miss Hume was amused.

Alexia allowed him a faint smile, and said, pursuing her
own point, "I don't know that there are many women now-
adays who would put up with a love affair. It's very demanding . . . very confining. Marriage allows one much
more freedom. I would never be anybody's mistress."

"What do you think, doctor? Do you think love affairs
are romantic?" Miss Hume asked.

To the extent that Gerard had heretofore thought about

love affairs actually in the flesh, they had seemed to him sordid, not particularly on moral grounds but because of the sneaking in the back doors of hotels. Now he felt a pang at the idea that they might be passé, that they'd had their golden moment but he'd slept through it. He considered what to say to Miss Hume, getting points by his silence for being very wise.

"Well, you may be right, Virginia," Alexia said, saving him from having to find an answer. "There's a great market in nostalgia. I only meant that with no more rules to break . . . and the ubiquitous porno . . . it all militates against the *probability* of a grand passion. But suppose the setting were hospitable. Not Washington, but what about Boston?" she asked, turning to Winters with an encouraging smile, as though he might be pleased that she had found a way to put Boston on the map, that although it was a hundred years behind they might make it into a kind of national trust of illicit passion.

Winters was pleased. "Certainly makes it more interesting to get back there," he said.

Miss Hume was not pleased. She did not write historical romances she said and she thought Alexia gave herself airs. "I might, Alexia, add," she added, "that you may have your finger on the Washington pulse, but I've only known two people who live there, both women, and they've both had affairs, one of them for twenty-five years!"

"Yes," said Alexia, with the confidence of giving a satisfactory answer. "It certainly seems harder to get out of an affair than a marriage."

Gerard laughed, although Alexia clearly meant to be

taken at her word, and Miss Hume did not laugh.

"If it were my book . . ." said Alexia, pausing for a moment to consider.

"Do you write, too?" Winters asked.

"She doesn't do anything," said Miss Hume.

"I write a little," said Alexia.

"She doesn't do anything much," said her aunt.

"I would have a heroine," Alexia resumed, "who falls in love and decides to marry and have children and live happily ever after. Now, ironically, you'll think that's very romantic."

"Well, it certainly hasn't been done *lately*," said Miss Hume.

"Until death do them part, a very carefully considered decision. It would be a *feminist* novel," Alexia pursued. " 'Do you take this man to be your lawfully wedded husband, for better and for worse, etc., etc., until death do you part?' 'I do!' she would cry out. That would be the great climax."

Miss Hume, not liking her leg pulled, took a deep and audible breath. Gerard thought Alexia looked serious and even somewhat oracular.

"You may breathe, Virginia, but it will have been a tremendously sophisticated, a most avant-garde decision," said Alexia, prophesizing. "A most studied choice. Pandora . . . I would name her Pandora. She has been sitting by her chest, very beautiful. She's been sitting there for years, now crossing one leg, now the other, through her childhood, through her girlhood, until she's about thirty. The lid of the chest is up, and flying in and out of it at leisure, and around her head, are little furry gray bats—the domino theory, the divorce rate, bourgeois anomie, oil spills, non-biodegradable plastic, pornography, Billy Graham, speed, Nixon, *et alii*—who are limp creatures with the mange. But unlike the original Pandora, the first woman, whom Zeus made silly and vain and who flung up her hands and screwed up her face at what she'd done, this Pandora is very cool. She knows where it's at, as they say, and she's considering her options, as they also say."

"They also say 'life styles,' " said her aunt with a small moue.

"Yes, well, it would certainly be better if you wrote it, as I, of course, never will. You wouldn't have to call her Pandora. But anyway the point is that she will have had every variety of woman under her purview, every sort of sexual and marital arrangement, and that's the part you could flesh out so well, Virginia . . . so that when she finally chooses the historic indissoluable marriage it will seem like the wildest kind of *nouvelle vague*, radical acting-out . . ."

"It sounds more like *Pilgrim's Progress* to me," said Winters.

"I never liked Pandora," said Miss Hume.

"*Pilgrim's Progress*, then," said Alexia. "And on the way there would be chapters called 'The Mistress,' 'Vermont Commune,' 'In the Closet,' 'Out of the Closet,' 'Divorced Wife,' 'Second Marriage,' and for each there would be a candid, *nonjudgmental* characterization . . ." She looked at her aunt doubtfully as though to wonder, after all, whether she could handle the subject.

"What about an example?" Winters asked.

"Well, I've already roughed in the mistress, but all right,

for another instance, take the woman who thinks she's unhappy because she's married to a fool. And so she divorces
him, and marries somebody else. For my part, my heart has
a quiver for a person in that situation . . . the idea that she
must wake in the middle of the night and say, 'My God!
I did it again! How could I have done it twice?' "

"So that it's better to marry once and for all," said
Winters, "because otherwise you're destined to repeat your
mistake? You're right, it isn't the most romantic testi-
monial."

He continued to be amused, and Miss Hume continued,
annoyed. "You can't really be against divorcing a fool,
Alexia."

"No, but it has its pitfalls. Anyhow, it isn't something
you head toward, when you're sitting by your chest considering what you're going to do and you haven't made
your first move yet. If you marry in the first place it's because you don't want to be lonely, you want to be part
of the historical and biological flow. But it is notable that
women who do get divorced find themselves sucked into
another marriage the moment they are free . . . as if by
some cosmic vacuum cleaner . . ."

Gerard watched as Alexia and her aunt batted the ball
back and forth, deliberately casual, Alexia protesting that
she was not, after all, talking about love and happiness but
about strategy, "or what you prefer to call choosing a 'life
style,' Virginia," and concurrently he listened, and he felt a
rising attraction to that impassive and cool beauty, and he
defended a counterstrategy—how else to secure a woman
with such an indifferent view of one's passion except with

barbed wire? He thought it would be awfully interesting to take a look at that husband to whom she had, one was led to believe, made the enduring vow. Was he satisfied? Could he rouse her? Had he regularly to bind her up? And when, after a while, he caught sight of Kitty coming down the hill with Cass—stolid, familiar, unexotic Kitty—Gerard wondered whether Alexia could ever possibly be somebody's old shoe?

They needed two minicabs for the ride back. In the one, Gerard said, in a voice that conveyed the intention to register a rebuke while pretending not to register a rebuke, that he hoped the girls were all right. "You mean not abandoned in the quarry?" Kitty asked, turning back on him, but in the best of humor. She was feeling much, much better. And the thought flitted across his brain that he had said something small, so mechanically, that it could hardly be said to have an intention after all.

In the other cab, Cass turned abruptly to Virginia and said, "You know, my girl, I think Mimi's recovered. The old man was quite right. Change of air. Trip's done wonders for her. Now just this morning she was talking to me about Aeschylus and the *Oresteia* and the design of this proscenium here with the greatest mental competence. Sound as a dollar."

"In English? Was she talking in English?"

"French."

"Sound as a franc," said Virginia pointedly. The franc had been very erratic that week. There was speculation whether they would let it float.

"Listen, Virginia, the vast majority of mankind finds

one language ample. Let her alone. What I was thinking of doing was . . ."

"Bolting."

"Taking the plane from Catania."

"Out of the question."

"How the hell have I got myself back to Taormina?" he growled.

Eight

I<small>N</small> Catania the bus passed a lava bed deposited by an old eruption of Etna. It was the first sight of lava the passengers had. The children, publicly, found it ugly and disappointing, the adults privately. Beyond Catania the route to Taormina lay along the Ionian Sea, which was a shimmery white in the late afternoon and undemanding in the way of attention. Winters gazed into it, silent, his mind engaged altogether elsewhere.

"You are so pensive. What are you thinking about?" Kitty asked in a tone that invited friendly intimacy.

"Oh, the usual—God, immortality, duty," Gerard said, friendly in turn.

"That's an old chestnut," she said, correcting his tendency to excessive admiration.

"You know what Cass told me?" he asked, skirting the correction. "Cass said the pebbles on these beaches are very large and they're called pobbles."

Kitty sensed a rebuff and said, "Do you know what Cass

told me? Cass told me our hotel was Nazi headquarters during the war." It was the San Domenico Palace Hotel and she had already said that during the Middle Ages the Dominicans were the most fanatical inquisitors of all.

Gerard drew breath, all set to return the volley when the bus unexpectedly came to a short full stop, took a sharp left, and in low gear began a heavy, grinding climb up the long, steep grade, around the hairpins, up and up, and finally through the gates of the beautiful medieval town of Taormina.

The San Domenico Palace in Taormina was the seventh most magnificent hotel in the world. By leaning over the balcony of his room high above the Ionian Sea, Gerard Winters could see to the far left the Greek amphitheater (which was Roman) cresting the head of the old town. By sitting back in his woven metal lawn chair he had the grand panorama of the snow-covered Mount Etna on his right, with its smoke puffing up into the blue sky. By being at this hotel at all he'd annoyed Kitty. Hundreds of millions of impoverished people all over the world could not afford to stop here. Strictly speaking, Winters couldn't either. And there were many very good alternative choices. But borrowing Virginia Hume's terms, he explained himself to himself by saying that every once in a while, intuitively, he had attempted to relieve the very plotlessness of their lives, in this instance by buying his family four Arabian nights with the *haute bourgeoisie*. He could not have been more delighted with himself.

Not more delighted since Cass and his women were staying here too, although where, along the miles of elegant corridors, they were quartered he had not yet discovered. For themselves, the Winters commanded a handsome suite, so that even John was appeased by a kind of small sitting room with a bed and a table to work on and his own balcony—sullen John who had not sat with Alexia this last leg, be it noted.

From the moment of the fiasco of chianti, Winters had listed toward Cass and his women as though something were the matter with his wheel. Or, to change the analogy, they beguiled him, like a band of gypsies, with their variegated scarves and intellectualisms, their casual linkage one with another, so uninstitutionalized, so free-swinging: he was easily seduced to hop on their painted wagon. By comparison he felt himself immensely unexceptional, unadventurous, predictable, accounted for: craven. Or, to bring the analogy back to Odysseus again, this was Sicily and this may have been where the Sirens sang.

He listened. When Virginia Hume talked about the kind of civilized people they all were, even though she was ironic, deprecatory, she endowed his own Boston—sometimes his own "unreal city"—with sophistication, with urbanity, even with lively possibilities. It had never been in his compass to consider an actual love affair, for instance. With whom would he have had a love affair? Not with a nurse, certainly. There was something shabby to him in those casual liaisons he knew to exist at the periphery of his awareness, shabby, and he was too *little* the male chauvinist to take that sort of advantage of his position. So that marital fidelity had always been to him a matter of aesthetics in combination with good citizenship. And the marriage itself was solid. There had been scenes, but they weren't scenes in a wasteland—by no measure were they that—and there had been no shrieking.

Down to his bones Winters did not like scenes. He couldn't remember when in these later years he began to say less and less of substance in an effort to avoid provoking them, or prolonging them. He was born into the belief that marriage must be an open partnership and, fantasies apart, was worthy of fidelity by a rational, self-disciplined, honorable, responsible, affectionate man. For the more than three years that he was a medical corpsman in the Ninth Army in World War II his fortitude grew great from feeding upon a vision of the worthiest and most companionable of futures side by side with the waiting Kitty. It was a cleaving vision, his love and his protecting arms wrapped around her love and her protecting arms. Twenty-five years into that future he was still a rational, self-disciplined, honorable, responsible, affectionate fellow as well as, and at his worst, managerial, insensitive, intrusive, presumptuous, from the point of view of his balking wife. And twenty-five years into that future he was still an unreflecting monogamist, and by forestalling as many scenes as possible, by, as far as possible, not hearing what Kitty might have said in them, he never really caught the theme of her recent distress. He was therefore surprised and hurt when sometime after the last of their children was born she said—quietly—that he oppressed her, that she felt suffocated, needed space. "You're always way over on my side of the line," she had said.

Although he really didn't know what she was talking about, he thought of himself as carefully backing off. When she announced her intention of returning to school, he moved in to clear the way for her, threw his shoulder to support the change, and sincerely believed that he gave her all the space she wanted. Last year, when she had put in twin beds—"You're always on my side of the line," she had said again—his approach to her, not easy in one bed, became all the more awkward.

Not only would this man say that he loved his wife, he would have to say more. Through time she had taken on portentous meaning, had become transformed from a fellow mortal to a sort of embodiment of values, of treasured and historical and earthly values, like one's birthplace or family homestead, or like one's books in one's own bookshelves, altogether inextricable, unsubtractable from what one is. Of course, he would take care of her if she were sick, stand by her when she was old, be there if she needed him; she was his place. And, of course, running around the place were the children and the memory of children. Were he to have known that Kitty had seriously considered subtracting herself, that she thought their union was indeed soluble, that she could and would consider herself an independent element, it would have wrenched him cruelly.

So it was that in spite of Kitty's prickliness, which he put down to hormonal changes, he thought of his marriage as simply good and solid, and he thought that Kitty's angry talk about feeling secondary and derivative, and her intention to become primary and autonomous, was a justified indictment of cultural forces hostile to women, and after a while, impossible to listen to.

Even the sanest man totters along the edge of two views of himself. Either he has missed the boat, or he has the best of all possible berths on these uncertain seas. That he had the best of things was wonderfully fortified by the sorry example of others. He may have been naïve about love affairs, but in cardiology, in the clinic, among the nurses, among the doctors, among the cleaning women, divorce was epidemic. His oldest friend and fellow cat-cutter, Andy Levinson, whose own marriage did indeed feature much shrieking and occasionally even the threat of murder, believed that a man who leaves home is destined to repeat the disaster at the cost of doubled tuition bills, a rousing endorsement of monogamy in a class with Alexia's. But Gerard's complacency on this matter was almost casually disturbed, not by Kitty and her demands to talk things out frankly, put everything on the table, which he would not talk and would not put, but by a stranger on a plane. It was about a year ago when he was flying to Richmond that he'd head the long story of a man who owned a chain of laundries in Providence, Rhode Island. He was a beefy lug, about fifty, with grown children, and his wife had given him one terrible time, he said, accusing him of everything, never willing to be happy about anything. Well, finally, after years of standing on his head spitting nickels, as he put it—and against everything he thought was right—he got a divorce. Meanwhile there was this woman, a branch manager . . . and the long of it was he remarried. Well, poor devil, he had evidently to talk about it to everybody all the time: he was very, very happy. "I look across the breakfast table," he said with actual tears in his eyes, "and I don't see somebody waiting ready to cut me down. It makes me goddamn *humble* . . ." he said, ". . . this *friendliness*."

It had not been his sexual fantasies that were excited, in

a man like Gerard who kept them under barbed wire, but his self-pity. He decided that he was lonely. News of the friendly love of an uncritical woman unsettled him. And now on the first morning of their sojourn at the San Domenico Palace he said to himself that it was not really Alexia who had him snorting and stamping in the winter cold of his balcony, it was the whole Cassagrande lot of them. But actually it was Alexia, and he went off, single-mindedly, through the narrow streets and alleys of the Middle Ages looking everywhere for her.

He found her. There were tables outside a restaurant in the cold sunshine and she was sitting quietly in her chair with her hands folded, like Whistler's mother, while her father, pivoting from his buttocks, read the lesson with great energy and humor to an attentive circle. Virginia Hume, eyes raised, arms crossed, was there, in her permanent state of not being taken in. Kitty was there, John was there, and Winters had some chagrin for their having got the jump on him. They were all drinking Campari for breakfast. Cass had a stack of saucers in front of him. Alexia had a white scarf on her head, a white scarf and black coat with a military collar, bringing her, on second thought, a shade closer to Napoleon than to Whistler's mother, counting the boots.

"We wondered whether you would find us," she said, sounding pleased that he had.

"Cass is fascinating about men, really very sharp," said Kitty, not seeming overpleased. Gerard, satisfied to disturb his wife a little, sat down by her side from which it was natural to look straight at Alexia, and asked where were the children? Alexia said that they had gone with Mimi to find the public gardens. She made it sound very interesting. He soon had his own drink, and Cass resumed an argument from the middle.

"Take your average man," said Cass. "Fellow who's been lucky," he qualified. "Likes his job, makes a little money, loves his wife, children, etcetera. Into a bit of reading: Marx, Darwin, Freud, *Times, New York Review,* little porn on the q.t. Pokes around the world from time to time, picks up a few things, few amber pieces, some first editions, English water colors . . ."

"By God! Straight out of middle America—a cross section," Winters said, laughing.

"*I'm* your average man," said Cass in a roar, defending his thesis.

"I find it difficult to believe that your life can be an illustration of any theory of human behavior whatsoever," said Virginia Hume.

"Puts his money where his mouth is; Gene McCarthy, Bobby, McGovern, all losers," Cass continued, happily disregarding his hecklers. "See these fellows everywhere, responsible, salt of the earth. And d'you know what they are?"

"Melancholy?" Winters was inspired to ask.

"Melancholy!" he affirmed. "And do you know why? Biharis in Bangladesh? Kids on horse? Arab terrorists?"

"No," said Gerard agreeably.

"The last time we met your fellows they were sitting in the jungle telling dirty stories," said Virginia Hume.

"No!" Cass repeated, ignoring her. "No. Unsatisfied wives!"

"For heaven's sake, what a fuss," Virginia said, shifting

her eye from one skeptical view of Cass to another. "That's the oldest story in the world."

"Ah, but of course I'm talking about a modification, my dear, if you'll just bear with me. The result of the liberation of women is that they've left off being abandoned themselves. *They're* walking out! It's the men who are being abandoned and this has exposed an ancient home truth lurking at the darkest corner of the hearth. It's the men who are monogamous by nature, in fact. And the women, in fact, who are not!"

"Come on, Cass," said Winters. "If you're going to be *my* average man you've got to admit to some degree of self-denial, *some* credit is due to . . ."

"I don't give more credit to a man than a woman," Cass said.

"Absolutely not!" said Kitty with an enthusiasm Gerard found unseemly in the extreme.

"What do you call yourself," Virginia asked, "a monogamist *manqué?*"

"I'm just your average humble observer," said Cass, looking like Churchill for the moment, and about as humble, "but all the yapping of the machos sounds to me like panic in the ranks. Any fellow, young or old, ask him privately, with no witnesses, does he want to swap the whole wild-oats business, all that highly touted taste for variety, turn it in for a steady household and a woman glad to see him come home every night, and he might just break down and cry. Trouble is that woman doesn't *stay* glad. She's got a lot of domestic instincts, and she's got a lot of undomestic instincts."

"I couldn't agree with you more," said Kitty in a voice

of heartfelt endorsement her husband felt he had rarely had the pleasure of hearing. "But it's impossible to point it out. They put their arms around you, give you a pat to set you straight, let you know fidelity's been at the painful price of one cold shower after another and what a struggle it's been to contain their particular superurges . . ."

Gerard, who had not been taking Cass's proposition seriously, was simply nonplused by Kitty's matter-of-fact support of it. "What the hell kind of nonsense are you talking, Kitty? Just who the hell is it who's taking all those cold showers?" he shot out at her.

"Andy Levinson, for one. When Eleanor was going to leave him and he was so upset. I was trying to help him to . . ."

"Eleanor was going to *leave him!* Never! If anybody was going to leave anybody, it was *Andy* . . ."

"Oh, that was just a love affair," said Kitty dismissively, dismissing a body of information and intelligence concerning Gerard's closest friend and colleague about which he, Gerard, knew little and believed less.

"Of course, it's the women who are walking out," said Cass, "and the men, poor devils, dazed, bitter, can't make out what's going on. Victims of their own miserable myth."

"I do think men are the victims," said Alexia reflectively.

"Antaeus!" said Cass. "Got to touch that home base, that woman, that's where his strength comes from. Antaeus—mind, heart, soul, body—needs that base because from that base he can spring out into the world, make his fortune, whatever. No good without it! That's his myth and that's his truth."

"He doesn't think about it," said Kitty all flushed and triumphant. "He just takes it for granted and we grant it."

"A woman has a lot of time to think," said Alexia, very calm. "A man hasn't the time. He isn't the thinker."

Alexia's pronouncement sounded to Gerard's ears very flattering, very supportive.

"I'd just like to know one thing," said John suddenly, speaking for the first time. His father had forgotten he was there. "I'd just like to know, if everybody's so equal, why a woman doesn't need a home base as much as a man? I'm telling you that women today are ready to . . . do anything, but when it comes to marriage, no way! That home base is just exactly what they don't want any part of. Talk about marriage, you blow it, you don't stand a chance. They're going to law school or they're going to med school and they want to keep everything open, everything good and fluid. Man, I wouldn't be in Sicily this minute . . . Sicily is the last goddamn place I'd be if it weren't for . . ." His anger had carried him this far, and he stopped, and there was a waiting silence, so he plunged on, ". . . this really fantastic woman who loves me, who's ready to move in, but she draws the line at commitment. Well, I got so goddamn mad . . ." He looked up, but everyone seemed expectant, as though he hadn't finished, so he repeated sullenly, "I just like to know why she doesn't need that goddamn home base."

"Ah, we hang between," said Alexia the prophetess quietly. "Between myths, between truths."

Gerard thought it was a soothing sort of thing to say

to his son, whatever it meant, but later when he and John walked back to the hotel together, John had found none of it soothing.

"I'll be damned if I'll be called monogamous," he grumbled, and slid into a sullen silence. He broke it, finally, by returning to the entirely different issue of why he wanted to marry Lisl—so that she would be reassured, so that there would be no doubt in her mind that he meant to renounce all others.

Nine

KITTY was blooming. Stimulated by Campari for breakfast, by brash talk, her skin turned taut and tawny in the kind winter light, and her manner turned confident. She and Alexia had gone off through the town in stride, long-legged, trim-tailored, and when they walked into the hotel toward lunch, a normal observer might have checked off two fine-looking women. Gerard, in all innocence, saw only one. Against the other he had a case building. He felt himself somehow being shouldered by Kitty on this third day in Sicily, as though she were competing with him in some awful personality contest, and winning. There was a particular irony in that, he thought, because it was she who had once accused him of having a competitive attitude toward her. He had never gotten over his indignation but avoided giving the subject another round.

After lunch, upstairs, neither of them at first said a word, he because of putting his grievances in order with an eye to the best opener. But she opened.

"John is just like you! It's amazing," she said with a trace of false enthusiasm.

Gerard had been finding some satisfaction that John *was* after all like him. John was not, in this event, part of his case against Kitty, and very decently he suspended his annoyance with her for the moment in order to reassure her, parent to parent.

"I wanted to tell you about John," he said. "We had a long talk this morning. I wanted to tell you that there was none of the bravado, the pretentiousness—he's in an awful lot of pain. He's in love with Lisl and wants to marry her . . . and she won't have him."

Kitty said nothing, seeming to resist his reassurance. Gerard became more earnest and true: "What I thought you'd like to hear is how decent a fellow he really still is, what a decent sort of quest he's on. He admitted finally that the whole wild-oats thing, as Cass calls it, really turned him off. He says he couldn't have been more surprised about himself. But he knew what he wanted. He wanted one serious, permanent, lifelong relationship. What his own parents had . . . marriage, a family. At the same time he speaks seriously of being glad to have Lisl go into law."

"I hear his father's voice," Kitty said, not in anger.

"Well, that's fine. I'm testifying to his good character . . . Anyway, Lisl seems, evidently, willing to share his bed and board, but she will not marry him."

"So I gathered. Poor Lisl."

"Poor John! He won't, as he says, shack up with her. That's why he's here—you heard him. He just wants that exchange of vows. He's an old-style romantic."

"Like his father."

"Well, it's comforting to know he isn't dishonorable, isn't it?"

"I just think that he and you are perfect illustrations of what Cass was talking about—domestic, family-minded *males*."

She spoke in a mild and reasonable way as if she were not scoring points at all. But it was a patronizing remark, besides being a silly one, from Gerard's view and he snapped, "I thought you thought Cass was full of hot air!"

"No, I don't think so."

"What happened to your pasha with the three horse-feathers?"

"I was mistaken."

"I'll tell you what else you're mistaken about. Andy Levinson. He was just a hairbreadth from walking out on Eleanor, a hairbreadth."

"That's not the way it was, Gerard. It was Eleanor," said Kitty, who continued to want to seem reasonable.

"You mean she found out about . . . that other business? There wasn't any other business."

"No, it wasn't *that* other business."

"Well, then why the hell would she want to leave Andy?"

Kitty, who had been putting things in drawers, straightened up, sighed, looked him in the eye, and said, "She was going to leave him because he said 'Eleanor, you can get more leaves than that in the leaf bag' once too often."

Gerard was not in the mood for snappy answers. "What makes me so goddamn mad, Kitty, is the way you trivialize your own side. I wouldn't mind so much if you thought Eleanor was ready to walk out because of another woman . . ."

"I call that closer to trivial."

He kept his temper and said, a little unctuously, even to his own ears, "As a matter of fact, there was no other woman. I think we ought to get that straight right now, out of a decent respect for another man's name."

"You know, when it comes right down to it, Gerard," she said, closing in predictably, "you have the blindest sort of male ego. You really don't even hear the words out of your own mouth. You seem to think it is the man's prerogative to walk out, and the noble men don't and that is how you can tell they're noble, if they restrain themselves. Well, in the first place there's a lot of brag there—all that repression a *man* has to manage because of his extramarvelous instincts. One always has to give him a lot of credit for keeping the lid on. And in the second place, millions of women keep the lid on without boasting and broadcasting, and moreover, and *notwithstanding*, there're about fifty compelling reasons why women get fed up with marriage and sex is the fiftieth!"

"Ha! Well, right there you've put it your way, just said it more crudely, that's all."

"Goddamn it, that's not what I mean. And I hate the smirking. I'd rather see a good, clean love affair than a dirty smirk."

"And for that matter, I don't think love affairs are all that trivial, Kitty." He stopped smirking.

"Oh, I don't think they have to be trivial," she said in a mocking voice; but then softening, she went on, "If you would only listen to what I say, but you don't. You assume you know what I'm going to say and then triumphantly you refute something I wasn't even talking about."

She never made allowances for how repetitive she could be, he thought, but forebore to mention.

"What I mean," she continued, "is that a woman may be just as liable as a man to have a love affair. After all, if she weren't, there'd be a shortage, and I don't hear of any shortage. And she's certainly as liable to physical excitability as he."

Gerard sincerely believed that Kitty had moved into a subject about which she was so underinformed as to make rendering an opinion an embarrassment. The implication that she was a student, theoretical and practical, of these matters, he would have to, in all charity, let go.

"The thing men don't understand about a woman's situation," she said with a little defiance, as though she spied Gerard's charity readily enough and would receive it the way most charity is received. "The thing they don't understand is that it's nearly impossible for her to make a move, even an innocent move, even writing a check for ten dollars to the Home for Wayward Girls, without being observed, weighed, judged, corrected. Really, her temptation to duck out, to find a secret friend, to steal something private for herself without *explaining*, without *defending* . . . may become nearly irresistible. After all, somebody who's always wonderfully well taken care of, provided for, seen to . . . well, it seems to me sooner or later it will send her right up the wall! I mean it seems to me perfectly understandable," she continued more forcefully, and provoked no doubt by the look of sovereign superiority on the face of her benefactor, "that if the right chance came along she'd be bound to grab it! Take it! Cut out!"

"Really, Kitty, sometimes you say things that are not only illogical but preposterous. Are you trying to tell me that you've felt so observed, so accounted for, that it's driven you into a love affair?" The idea was so preposterous to Gerard as to make his expression a little lunatic. He was two moments behind seeing that this was insulting to Kitty.

"That's coarse," she said finally, and set her jaw.

"Well, in good conscience," he said in what he thought was a retreat, "I think I've always given you all the freedom you want. As soon as I knew what you wanted, it was yours."

"Oh, Gerard, what delusions you let yourself keep. Freedom! *One*, not without a struggle, and *two*, it isn't yours to give. You were very resentful when I went back to school and you made it as difficult as possible . . ."

"That's not true! I supported you a hundred per cent! I just asked you whether you didn't think you ought to wait a couple of years until Vicky was . . ."

"That's exactly what I mean. I was forty-five years old, the mother of six children. Don't you think I had been all over that territory myself? You put nearly intolerable pressure on my conscience and then you deny that you curtailed my freedom."

"It wasn't intolerable, obviously. And I certainly did not curtail your freedom. If my memory is correct, I opened a new account for you next morning, and transferred eight thousand dollars into it and I didn't give a damn what you did with it!"

"You still don't know what I'm talking about, do you?"

She was now shouting in this scene. "You just can't hear what I mean. I don't want to be supervised! I can't stand it! I want to be all grown up without having to bring everything for higher approval. And John's just like you. He wants Lisl to sign up, write her name in blood, but she damn well won't do it! Well, cheers for Lisl! And cheers for Kate, too. I hope she digs her heels in."

Kitty had now crossed the line. There was a line before which Gerard felt himself vaguely culpable of committing unspecified misdemeanors, and by driving Kitty over the line he found himself immensely justified and wonderfully relieved of blame. It was the rare woman who could conduct an argument properly, who wouldn't strike out wildly. That their Kate, or for that matter somebody else's Lisl, or any girl, should be encouraged to look with contempt upon marriage, children, from all of which Kitty herself would not deny she had benefitted, seemed to him shoddy, not worth his time talking about. And now Kitty grabbed her coat and, as if it were her title, was the one to flounce out.

Once more Gerard was alone in his superior position. He walked over to the French window that gave out on the balcony, leaned his forehead against the cold glass, and was aware, not for the first time, that his reward for winning was a flattened spirit, a stale taste, an inevitable headache, and for these reasons he was on the very edge of becoming less obtuse about his moral certainty. For over fifty years people remained somehow unimproved, not the better for it. As he aged, all the forms that expressed his fine ethical sense were imperceptibly becoming fossilized and mechanical, and in particular the debating-society rules by which

he was fair, and fairly defeated Kitty; but she wasn't fair
and pretended he had not. These forms had not changed,
not been revitalized, although it was his own impression
that he could be extremely flexible, that he'd shown a
broad tolerance toward his older children, for instance, and
their godforsaken life styles, at the price of disguising—he
thought he was disguising—the bitterness and pain of seeing them make what he privately felt were vulgar choices.

The two older girls had refused the invitation to come to
Sicily, Kate evidently because she would not leave the bed
of the boyfriend, and Mary who would not leave the
shrink. A modern father, he had been superbly casual about
this, but privately he was outraged, in particularly about
Mary, that she would see a psychiatrist in the first place.
Why, he had asked, why was she seeing a psychiatrist? Because she wasn't happy! Well why the hell wasn't she
happy? The shrink said she had suppressed her emotions.
The fatuity of this remark was so evident it made him
laugh. The shrink was out of his own bloody mind, he said
to himself, a remark that nonshrinks need to make from
time to time. He riffled through his memories of Mary
when she was a little girl and saw smiles that were so
cheerful, saw such a busy participator with a real relish for
life, so expectant, and how like Annie was to her. Repressed, indeed! And then he slapped down his trump card.
What was the matter with repression? Repression was magnificent, what built civilization; it was the way you got
through.

From the French window and across the balcony railing,
all that could be seen were the blue sky and the whitening
afternoon color of the sea over whose surface Io had been

driven, chased by the gadfly, tormented. Although Gerard reminded himself to rejoice that this was the Ionian Sea and not the Charles River, and that repression was magnificent and built civilizations, he was crushed when he thought his beloved Mary unhappy. He would have pounded the glass against such an arbitrary fact, altogether without cause, if he had not been that model of restraint. And Kate, who had used part of the room-and-board money to live off campus with the b.f., how she had offended his sensibilities, he thought, how she had dropped her sights, had become part of the commonalty, had not held herself in reserve in spite of the high standards which were the only standards she had known from birth. And where the hell was causation? What the hell happened to the theory of causation? he asked himself.

But even as he railed against the failure of the system to hold up and be fair, he knew that he thought Kate, the b.f. notwithstanding, was in good shape, a solid citizen, and from there it was a small step to acknowledging that even while he was reassuring Kitty in the matter of John's honorable character, preening about the chip—the old block himself rang very hollow. Even to the defensive father the son's rectitude was narrow, self-pitying. And it sounded to him as though John were acting more like Achilles sulking because he couldn't have the girl who was his trophy (Homer), like Darius demanding earth and water as symbols of submission (Herodotus), than that he was revering Lisl's good name (Cary Grant) or upholding any principle from which Lisl was likely to benefit (Gerard Winters).

Ten

Winters found himself sitting in his room in a wilted condition with the daylight hours slipping by, which offended his Calvinist sense of economy. Abruptly he pulled himself together, picked up his coat, and set off. His fine character was rewarded. Literally he bumped into Alexia, just missed knocking her to the ground. On his way downstairs he had been striding with determined energy out from one dark corridor as had she from another. A fortuitous collision. They laughed, righted each other, and continued together along the quarter mile of carpeted floors and tapestried walls, through salons of potted palms and portraits, past maids with white furbelows, bellboys with brass buttons, socially superior stewards, and lesser guests, down the empty hallway where the old nuns' cells gave off, and finally out into the shadowy square. It was a big hotel. Alexia, with a canvas sack slung over the shoulder of her military coat, her hands in her pockets, her determined stride, looked as though she might have been setting off to

Moscow with the French army. Certainly she was going in the wrong direction, taking a left instead of the right that led to all the points described in the guidebook. Gerard, very brash, took the left with her. Immediately they had moved behind the scenes of Taormina, up through a steep and stubby street, where motorbikes leaned against the old stone of unrestored buildings, and lines of washing criss-crossed from the upper windows. There was here and there a tiny shop, there were children running about, and every-where those sure-footed old women in black shawls with bulging string bags who did not turn their ankles. Gerard took Alexia's elbow to steady her.

She smiled at him quizzically but pleased and said what a nice coincidence it was, his going to the Castello too. He smiled. They continued upward, climbing a narrow flight of stone steps rejoining their road above the town. The road was bare of leaf cover and could be seen to slide back and forth down the mountain. Gerard, exhilarated, felt risen above his domestic cares up here among the mountain-tops. Etna looked much closer. Their own mountain, from beneath the summit, was almost as imposing, but it had no snow. The walk ahead promised to be long.

"It's a short cut," said Alexia. "My husband and I found it by mistake. We were here on our honeymoon. I don't think it will take us more than half an hour to get up but I wanted to see it again. I am romantic after all, am I not?"

"My wife calls me a romantic," said Gerard, who had not previously liked that tag at all. He thought of himself as a realist *tout court*, and he thought Kitty flattered her-self she was a realist mainly by disliking Wordsworth.

They walked side by side in silence. Alexia had no trouble keeping up with him, and he had no trouble letting her. He was a little winded. He wondered whether he seemed old to her, paunchy, and from time to time he pulled in his stomach to test the bands of steel. He watched her as casually as he could manage and he found himself amazed that she was the exact materialization of the vague creatures he had had to bind with his barbed wire. All those years ago when he had fallen in love with Kitty, he had been a little confused by himself. He had dreamed of a mysterious icy beauty and she had been unmysteriously pretty, at most; not what he had originally meant, not what he had had in mind. Alexia was what he had always had in mind, he now believed, charming himself with this discovery. Her fair, impassive brow, the glamor of green paint on her eyelids, and a certain detachment, especially when she wasn't making perfect sense, kept her at one remove from the unimaginative everyday world; and this impression grew as they climbed and the air thinned.

"I'm not sure that my coming up here with you can pass as a bona fide coincidence," he said, emboldened, as they were nearing the Castello where the air was thinnest. "I'm just following you, you know."

"But I wanted you to. That's the coincidence, don't you see? I didn't want to climb up here by myself, although I don't like to leave the others. They need a moderator."

"Is that so?" Gerard asked, surprised. "I would have said they were the picture of unflappability."

"That's recto," she said. "That's our formal group portrait. But on the back side, when we are constrained by circumstances . . . to be together too long, we all get to look pretty flappy. In fact, the problem is to keep Cass from flapping off entirely. He believes Mimi is cured. Virginia has talked to you about Mimi?"

"A little."

"Virginia is confident that sanity and insanity are two clearly defined sovereign states, and that all we have to do is trick Mimi back across the border, catch her out in English. Virginia's very proud of being sane. And Cass, Cass is just like his father . . . as though if one would only let nature take its course, that nature would correct all the things people find disagreeable. Of course, when he's philosophizing, when it isn't inconvenient to him person- ally, he's the first to point out that nature doesn't give a rap. Then he's the great Darwinian. Well, consistency is the last refuge of a scoundrel," she finished with a shrug of her shoulders.

"I think it's the hobgoblin of small minds."

"You're right. Virginia has, really, a *generous* mind, but when she is unnerved it contracts. Cass unnerves her. It was perverse of fate to bring them back to Taormina. They met here when they were young, you know, just before everybody made the irrevocable lifetime wrong choices, in Virginia's view. Bliss was it in that dawn to be alive, she likes to believe, but it was the spring of thirty-seven, and the dawn of World War II actually. There were the two sisters from Roanoke, Sophie-Virginia and Mary-Agnes. Cass married the other, my mother." Alexia hesitated and then she said, "Well then, my mother drowned when I was twelve and Mimi was ten. We never really knew what normal family life was like. It entitles Mimi to a lot . . . a lot of behavior."

She paused again, but since Gerard was not sure about

whom they were talking, he kept quiet, and so on she went.

"Poor Virginia. She took mother's death as evidence of a wrong choice. But by the same token she ought to have congratulated herself for not having married Cass and therefore not having had to drown herself. It's not reasonable to have it both ways. Do you think it's reasonable?"

Something wasn't reasonable. Gerard, made lightheaded by the climb and the altitude alone, without throwing in Alexia, turned their attention away from the question of what was reasonable and to the view from the Castello.

The Castello had been the site of a fortress farther back into history than could be determined and had last been repaired by the Saracens. Now there was almost nothing of the fortress left, but by leaning on its rubble they could see one of the finest views in Europe. The sky almost surrounded them, was almost palpable, and so clear that the deep blue molecules could be seen dancing into infinity. The valleys were already dark, with scattered lights, but beyond, the sea was still pale and the Straits of Messina were distinguishable between the two black lands of Sicily and Italy, where the sea monster Scylla waited brooding beyond the whirlpool Charybdis. Besides monsters and Sirens, heroes and Titans, there was not, apparently, a soul up here with them. The light was draining, the time was running out, and nobody knew where Gerard was. He was on top of the world.

There was even more view, more horizon, and Alexia remembered the path leading through stubble and debris, past the remains of a stone wall to the other side of the sky where Mount Etna presided, with her unencompassable breadth, over the whole world. Etna was not tall like an alp but vast and with a cover of snow, and coming out of the middle was the short wriggle of smoke dancing on its toe like a white eel. They were standing at the railing of a small terrace that was a tea garden in summer, and a few metal chairs and small tables had been left out. So they sat down to watch it get dark and get late. And Alexia explained that she was determined, in respect to her own children, two boys of eleven and six, that family life for them would be tranquil and secure. "I'm fiercely determined upon tranquility," she added, smiling, sitting back against the darkening sky and the mountain while seven swallows circled. By a trick of light she looked larger than life and her skin turned the color of chamois. She had a housekeeper, she said, but she took care of the children herself and made a point of always being at the door when they came home from school. What a mother, he thought, feeling as though he had just put away two wholesome high-protein martinis. The swallows swooped like bats. They might have been bats, and she might have been Pandora, Pandora with a greatcoat fortunately, since it was not only getting darker and later but colder. Suddenly Pandora stretched out her arms and said grandly, "I have been the president of the Parents Organization of the Sidwell Friends School."

She went on to explain that because her own mother had been a rather diaphanous creature, she herself was determined to be a solid presence in the household, absolutely dedicated, what they call family orientated, and then she added, casting a gaze across the horizon and with reference to her not being crouched by the hearth at this particular moment, "They let me have a breather from time to time."

"You don't want to be a fanatic," Winters said agreeably, laughing.

"Mimi reveres the family too. When you don't have one, then you revere it," she said, looking into the distance.

So much enthusiasm was irrational to Gerard, even in his present condition. "You know, Chekhov describes his family as being depressed by the abnormality of living together," he said, characteristically redressing a balance.

For the first time Alexia's wandering attention came to a halt. For the first time she looked at Gerard thoughtfully, narrowing her eyes a little, as though she were putting him up for reconsideration, as though some oversight might have been made on the first go-round. He was surprised at her surprise and felt almost that he was in touch with a real self.

This illusion did not survive their departure from the mountaintop in the now black, starry night and the zigzag descent to the town. There was no moon but the road was whitened by starlight, and Gerard once more yielded to the feeling that it was an extraterrestrial presence who was swinging her arms by his side.

"Have you read Proust?" she asked after a silence that lasted nearly to the town.

"When I was at college I read *Swann's Way*. It was more than I could manage at the time."

"I think one has to be past thirty. I always read Proust now. If you are interested in the abnormality of living together, you might try again. But you don't read French, do you? And curiously, it isn't funny in English. It's very comical in the original. And then, of course, it's very long,

and you say you are already fifty-three. Do you have lon-
gevity in your family?" She was laughing at him.

"My father and mother both died of it," he said. "And,
as a matter of fact, when I was fifty I thought since I only
had a half century left, that I'd put things in order and
start all over again—with Homer. So I'll get to Proust, but
not until I'm about eighty-seven."

"Well, you know, the other day," she said, "when we
were talking about love affairs, I ought to have reminded
Virginia of Swann's epitaph on his love affair with Odette.
It is, after all, remarkable for its crushing insight. People
know it by heart. One wonders why so many people know
it by heart . . . but you don't? . . . Well, loosely translated, he says, 'To think that I wasted years of my life, that
I've wanted to die, that my one grand passion was for a
woman who didn't please me, who wasn't my type.' I must
remember to tell Virginia."

Gerard had only a dim remembrance of Swann's hu-
miliating obsession and of his own complete lack of understanding. "You worry about the demise of the love affair
the way other people worry about the collapse of marriage," he said, "as though it were one of the sustaining
structural institutions of Western culture." He smiled at
her, stalled before the courtyard of the hotel, nervous about
the hour, unable to bring this to an end. Alexia was lit by
Christmas lights, which were wrought-iron scrolls sown
with colored bulbs that made beautiful winter bowers of
the narrow streets.

"Well, a love affair is more poignant, after all. Men and
women are always marrying people who are not pleasing to

them, who are not their type. So that classically, the love affair ought to have been the relief . . . ought to have made that small private amends for those ineluctable forces that funneled you through to the wrong choice. But, after all, see what happens to Swann," she said a little mournfully, her eyes wandering vaguely along the street.

"What happens to Swann?"

"Well, in the next book one discovers matter-of-factly that he *married* Odette, that after he was quite free of his sexual obsession, when he no longer had to blind himself to her awful bourgeois affectations, when he was all but indifferent to her . . . that then he married her. Really, it's very jarring when you learn of it. It's that ineluctability again. Maybe you won't want to wait until you're eighty-seven. Do you ever skip?" she asked, smiling too, sometimes as amused by his ways as he was by hers. He said doubtfully, half seriously, that he might skip, but as though he hadn't answered at all, she turned to look at him directly, and repeated in a not unkindly tone, "Do you ever skip? Do you ever break your own rules? Do you ever surprise yourself?"

Kindly tone or not, he was dismayed by her questions because in the first place his whole excursion to the Castello with her was strictly out of character, and in the second so was this shuffling about, this not hurrying back to check in and report. For hours nobody had known where he was. He was very late, although not very late for anything in particular. But he had broken his own first rule of accountability. So that in effect she'd only seen him when he was skipping, when he was surprising himself. The dismay must have been written on his face because she put out her hand to touch his hand, or rather glove upon glove, and said very warmly, "I must tell you that I've loved our walk, our coincidence, and I have a very respectful attitude toward coincidence. The moments are rare and fleeting when people come into phase, coincide in their pleasures. Like little truces . . . One ought to celebrate them."

Eleven

THREE days and nights in Taormina followed, during which the tour members developed such a sense of group identity, such a pride of vintage, that it was curious they didn't come to the attention of wandering anthropologists. Gerard Winters managed innumerable coincidences, again and again finding himself surprised to encounter Alexia, but never finding her alone. This was largely due to Virginia Hume's rather fanatical determination to keep Mimi in English-speaking company. Indeed, she felt that she alone had proposed a serious plan to deal with poor Mimi, who had, unexpectedly, turned gay and dreamy playing nurse-maid to the Winters girls, with her warders in collusion. She believed they, the warders, were reprehensible. Cass thought they'd achieved something. Nothing had been achieved, she had assured him, if Mimi still could not speak English, the clinical symptom. What would she do when she was back in Brussels? She could be a French governess,

Cass suggested, only half in humor. The other half wanted this problem dissolved by any solution.

Cass settled down to their spell in Taormina, about which he seemed to feel no nostalgia, resigning himself cheerfully to the adulation of his fellow tour members, scattering philosophical observations and favorite theories for the pleasure of the ladies in particular, saving the big guns for Kitty Winters. Rousing, zesty, expansive, spotting the best restaurants in town, he had all of them eating and drinking and ruining their livers, a regular jack-a-dandy, hail fellow, and fond father, superbly inattentive to Virginia's language instructions. Virginia was beginning to be tired of it.

"It seems to me you're getting bloated. I think you've taken on water," she said to him.

"Ridiculous! Tremendous vitality! Feel like a fellow of twenty-five!" he boomed. This she heard as sexual swagger, a red flag to her.

"You don't fear . . . apoplexy?" she asked him mildly.

He pondered her for a moment or two, and then assuming a bewildered look, said, "You're becoming a senior citizen, now, Virginia . . . *Quite* miraculous conversion."

"Well, it's confusing for *me*, you know, to look at *you* and think, 'Ah! That's where the sap's rising!' Take it *one* way."

He patted his pockets for cigarettes, lit one, let the smoke out, and said, "Don't suppose you remember Isak Dinesen's story of the flood?"

"Of course, I remember. *Deluge at Norderney*. The old woman and the cardinal are adrift in the flood and they're going to drown."

"Exactly," he said, bowing his head in honor of her well-stocked mind, and putting her on her guard. "A Miss Nat-og-dag of an illustrious family. One learns that she has been a lady of the *strictest* virtues throughout her life. And now we meet her as she is about to die, presenting herself to the cardinal as one of the great female sinners of her time, confessing to endless lustful adventures, relishing the details of every one of them." He stopped, looking pleased.

Virginia was properly wary. "Well?" she asked.

"Well, *you*, my dear, are Miss Nat-og-Dag stood upon her head. Don't you see it? One of the great female sinners of the . . . New Deal administration," he said, sweeping his arm grandly in deference. "You've gotten damn stuffy!"

She heard this for the most part as a piece of flattery.

Virginia could not seriously puncture Cass's complacency and in regard to Mimi, Alexia was as evasive as Cass. Alexia said she had spoken to Gerard Winters about Mimi's problem and whether some sort of relaxing medication might be indicated, and he had said it was not within his competence to suggest any. This, it seemed to Virginia, was another instance of evasion. "I call that sloth!" she snapped.

"That's not a very acute observation, Virginia," said Alexia mildly. And it wasn't. The doctor had been indefatigable in attending to the calls of his fellow passengers, no matter how trivial the concern, in what language it was described, what hotel, what time, and as often as he turned to Alexia for help in translation, Mimi trotted along to nurse; Virginia's contribution. Their second day in Taormina there was actually a case of an elevation in temperature, Mme Bontemps', and it was immediately the talk of the tour how Dr. Winters had read the thermometer, taken the pulse, prescribed two aspirin every four hours, and had her on her feet by the following morning.

After so superb a performance, it was natural that he should be consulted on such masculine matters as the purchase of donkey bells and puppets, that, by extension, Kitty's advice would be valuable about picnics, about choosing embroidered linens, that she, in turn, their chosen Ur-mother, should be urged to have her rosy children drink watered wine for the blood, or carry horseshoe nails in their pockets, also for the blood, and to the children themselves they brought every sort of candy and cake, regardless of their action on the blood or the stomach. All of these daily visits testified to the comfort people drew from simply checking in with the Winters, excepting Frau Fassbender of the bursitis, the holdout, the necessary pariah, who did not believe it was bursitis. When young John Winters disturbed the orderly progress of events by his determination to fly back to Rome, he asked Alexia, who had a rented car, whether she would be willing to drive him to the airport at Catania. But the doctor wouldn't hear of Alexia's driving back alone. He did not shirk his obligations. In the end, quite a party went to see John off. So that it was unjust of Virginia to call Winters slothful, and in fact, she forgot she had.

Cautiously, Virginia became fond of the children. One morning she walked up the narrow alley past La Rose-Thé, the pensione in which she had lived for three months more than thirty years ago, and which now, no matter how many times she had come to take a look at it, meant nothing at all to her. From the alley she knew how to slip into a wing of the amphitheater. It was late in the morning and the empty theater was a wide bowl of sunshine so yellow as to make it difficult for her to see, and the wind was freed up here to catch at trash and whip it around in twisters. Squinting, blinking, and puffing, she followed the paths of the cats up the steps toward the hot stone of the topmost protecting wall. It was several moments before she discovered she was being watched, and that along the wall, in each of three tall narrow niches for three goddesses there was a Winters child keeping still as a statue, holding her breath, her bellow ready to bound loose. When Virginia saw them, all these bellows of welcome did bound loose and they clambered down toward her, noisy and delighted with themselves. Then Mimi came out of nowhere clutching a greasy bag with *faione di ricotta*, and they all sat in a row in the sun against the curved top wall eating the fried pastries which was a certain way to produce heartburn. Below them was the stage, and rising above it for a tremendous backdrop was Mount Etna with its little puff-puffing of smoke.

The children ate and chattered in English, Mimi smiled in French, and Miss Hume capitulated to a conversation first in English and then in French and felt like Ina. The content was governed by the verb forms.

"Do you like this cake?" Oh, boy, didn't the girls just, and from Mimi something something sugar.

"Do you like to go to Mount Etna?" A volley of affirmative responses from the children, and Mimi saying she would regret strongly the end of the sojourn.

"Do you want better to go to Washington at the sister?" Miss Hume asked Mimi. Mimi thereupon frowned and her eyes wandered off to the puff of smoke. The trip to Mount Etna was the penultimate day when Ina and her bus were to haul them all up, and then down to Catania for the night, and next morning the plane back to Rome.

Annie said to Miss Hume, with extrahearty enthusiasm, as though to deflect the conversation away from Mimi, "Mount Etna! It saves the best for the last," And she stared earnestly at the sight of this pending adventure.

"If there isn't a torpedo!" said the smallest girl, mischief in her voice.

"A volcano!" the other two corrected.

Then Annie bent round to Miss Hume and explained, "Our father says there is no reason to worry about the volcano at all . . . and nobody is to worry about that smoke. Because there are scientific instruments that tell you three days ahead when there's going to be an explosion. So we have three whole days of warning. That's plenty of time."

"I'd just like to see with my own eyes a melted rock," said the middle sister, Elizabeth.

When they'd finished up the pastries, Elizabeth crumpled the empty bag and shoved it into her pocket. "Keep Sicily clean!" she announced, and laughed with delight at her own joke. They were awash in windblown trash.

"Mimi's taught us a lot of French," said Annie confidentially to Miss Hume, taking her hand, on their way back to the hotel. "Although all Vicky needed to know was 'J'ai faim!'" Another joke and more laughing. And Virginia Hume laughed.

But she was not diverted from her intention to force Mimi's re-entry into the real world of adults where they spoke the English language, so that when they all trooped into the hotel with an hour to go before lunch, and there were Alexia and the doctor heading for the bar, she offered Mimi and herself and the children for company. Mimi demurred. Winters sent the children to their rooms but did not send Virginia to her room, and so there was a general foiling of intentions.

Twelve

Fʀᴏᴍ the point of view of every one of the remaining
Winters (John having decamped) this trip was the best they
had ever had. Gerard, forever scheming to be off alone with
Alexia, was forever baffled. But suppose he had managed a
private rendezvous, what would he have said in it that he
wasn't able to say more easily in front of other people? Not
a damn thing. Contrariwise, by always being thwarted he
was kept happily titillated while at the same time out of
the danger of being misunderstood. He was not a man who,
in real life, made propositions to women. And his belief
that a man should not seduce another woman corresponded
tidily with his fear that he could not. So that while he was
frustrated, he was someone who had long since learned to
handle frustration, even enjoy it.

In fact he was exhilarated, rejuvenated, fending lightly
against guilt. The bonhomie with which he approached
Kitty one night, after a day in pursuit of Alexia, was com-
pounded of good spirit, and the necessity to dissemble, and

above all the need for her physically, which was where he entered an area of torment, an area not unfamiliar, however.

"What do you think about getting some Sicilian donkey bells for your mother?" he asked Kitty in his fondest voice, expecting particular credit for giving thought to the enemy.

"Oh, she doesn't give a damn about donkey bells. She doesn't even approve of Sicily," said Kitty indifferently. Her mother was Kitty's enemy, too.

"Sure," he insisted. "It's a good idea. She can nail them up on the front porch."

"Oh, I'll find something else. Doilies or something."

But Gerard, the archetype of the best American husband in this regard, always overvalued his own good ideas, and he pushed this good idea, pushed the donkey bells, with his characteristic insensitivity to Kitty's resistance. Kitty made a lot of lame excuses for not wanting the donkey bells and finally said they weren't going to be able to buy off her mother for not being with her at Christmas anyway, that she'd just talked to her and it was like talking to a martyr.

"You called her again? You just called her from Rome."

"She had a cold."

"She always has a cold. You know, we are going to be home Sunday. You might have waited until Sunday to let her slap you down. Jesus Christ, I don't really give a damn how much you spend. I simply think there're a lot more worthy charities to give your money to than ITT. How much did it cost?"

"I haven't any idea. I charged it to the room. And I'm not going to discuss it."

"Well, I don't know why you get so huffy about it. It seems to me I'm the one who . . ."

"I . . . will . . . *never* explain a phone bill again."

Gerard stopped, uncertain about which direction he wanted to go, and chose the bathroom. His annoyance about the telephone was more mechanical than deeply felt, all his deep feelings committed elsewhere, and now Kitty's turning sullen was one more hurdle on an obstacle-strewn road to love. Who to blame but himself for that? Thoughtless. But in the shower his unwonted effervescence resumed bubbling and he returned to the bedroom all forgive and forget and determined to run the course. Among the necessities in his life this was indeed the hardest, and his loins were girded.

The hushed gray-blue lamp-lit room could not have been more suggestive. The bed—a *lettò matrimoniale*—had been turned down on each side with mathematical neatness to form a pyramid of sheet, and there was still a little incense in the air from a candle the maids burned while they went their evening rounds. The whole family had been amused by these curious luxuries, the children admiring the incense in particular for its authentic hippitude. Annie was certain it was a clever way to satisfy that sort of guest and considered for a moment going into the hotel business. She thought the sheets were silk. Kitty said of course not, they were only ironed. Poor children didn't know what ironed sheets were. But Kitty was enjoying it all anyhow, and she said so, and had told Gerard, laughing at herself, that the true reason she ranted against all this sinful stuff was that she had such a taste for it. Even now, with her hair loose and in her nightgown, she sat by the dressing table, not sullen, smiling calmly at some inner thought, taking Gerard by surprise for not looking like an obstacle in any way.

Kitty was not an obstacle. Indeed, she had been inviting and Gerard, in a confusion of feeling, rolled back to his side of the bed thinking it had been a long time since they had come together with such pleasure. It had certainly been a long time since he had felt himself ratified, and gratifying, and he would have enjoyed letting his satisfaction expand if he hadn't had Alexia waiting in the wings of his nights. He proceeded to Alexia, to her re-evocation, but it was difficult. He had to swim against a great drowsiness.

"You know Alexia?" Kitty said out of the blue, or out of the sound sleep she was supposed to have been sunk in. "I think she calls her husband every afternoon at five. I don't mean I'm going to compete with her. I just thought it might broaden your perspective."

Gerard was properly startled, his perspective broadened. Kitty laughed and groped for his hand. "I'm sorry when I snap at you. It's because you're unregenerate. If you would just see where I am and take me straight, leave off being my guide and stay. You ought to listen to Cass. He really has a feeling for women, empathetic . . . not Virginia. He calls her the male chauvinist. I think we're awfully lucky to run into them. Don't you think they're stimulating? Are you asleep?"

"Not quite."

"Aren't they stimulating?"

"They really are." He was able to say that warmly.

"You know," she went on dreamily, "reading a history of Mediterranean culture and at the same time walking around in the middle of it—it's instructive, and really humbling in a way you'd never . . ."

She was off. Gerard half heard, and closed his eyes. At

this particular moment he found himself with the least trouble in the world, easily able to resist being humbled and instructed, and his mind spread out into the dark.

"I mean, as Cass points out, you simply have to conclude that the level of moral sophistication in *whole societies* was very immature. The swaggering, the ingenuous quality of the guile, the insane pomp at those princely courts, the excessive sensitivity to insult—I used to think Benvenuto Cellini was some sort of exception, but he wasn't! He really was a prototype, talk about machismo and the male ego! Why you would have to think twice even about a man like Erasmus, who was, after all, one of the most urbane . . ."

Gerard wondered if he could think about Erasmus once, while he let Kitty's words travel, quiet and orderly across his brain. He thought Kitty certainly was a much finer person than Benvenuto Cellini . . .

". . . and I suddenly feel, even if I know we're doomed, how magnificent, if I'm only going to live once, to have been born inside the American democratic experiment so that I've had a crack at . . . really *growing*, morally, intellectually, really 'catching on,' as Cass puts it. Now that's not romantic, is it? Do you think that's merely romantic?"

She caught him unprepared for comment. He scanned the possibilities and chose "No."

"No, it's not romantic. That's my actuality, my reality . . . and I've just been feeling what enormous luck it is to have been me, to have had my rich life . . . with you . . ."

She concluded a little sheepishly, he thought, suddenly overwhelmed by affection for her. It wasn't exactly what she said that brought him back to his own center, since he only half attended. It was the sound of contentment in her voice, her intelligence and decency so thoroughly familiar, so substantial and integral to her nature; and as beautiful as the part in her brown hair to his beholding eye. She had not finished. She was in full sail. He lay there holding her hand in a groggy peace, amused at himself for being so easily reclaimed, so readily reclaimable, and gave Cass A-minus for his theory of monogamy.

". . . when the children and I were waiting for you before dinner in that gorgeous salon with the crystal chandeliers and the potted palms and I was watching our fellow guests gather, so many overstuffed women with their awful taste—black-dyed curls and mink stoles and diamond jewelry, and their expressions so bored or petulant, so vulgar, so *inhumane*. They seemed left over from another era . . . as though we'd wandered into a scene in a movie out of the thirties and Groucho Marx would come loping in at any moment and drop ashes on some fat naked shoulder. Signora Piazza says they are the industrial *nouveaux riches*. They come from Messina. Well, you know, I had the strangest insight about myself. I thought, there but for the grace of God go I. What I mean is that before, when we were driving through those bleak villages and we saw so many old black *crones*, with their exhausted, toothless, hard faces and it occurred to me that a lot of those women who looked as though they could be my grandmother were probably *younger* than I was . . . well, I didn't think *then*, there but for the grace of God . . . but *these* people are not really all that remote. They're actually options I might have been. I mean to this day I would be the prodigal daughter if I came home with a mink stole and diamonds. My mother would take them for signs of repentance!"

"They were never your options, Kitty. You were always too fine, too wise, too . . . humane . . ." Gerard murmured, and meant, and it was about here through a seeping bliss that he must have fallen off to sleep the sleep of the acquitted.

In the morning he woke wanting her again. She lay on her back with her eyes open, with the same mild smile of the evening before, and he reached for her.

"Oh, darling, we just did that," she said, seeming amused.

"Well, let's do it again," Gerard said, feeling sure.

"It's not reasonable," she protested in a tone tapping his assurance.

"Its not supposed to be reasonable, and you liked it last night," he reasoned.

"I liked giving you what you wanted."

"That's all?"

"That's a lot."

"But you weren't . . . satisfied?"

"What can I do about that? It's simply physiological. You're a doctor. I don't know why you just can't understand, why it's so difficult for you to accept the second law of thermodynamics. Somewhere along the line people lose their physical sensibility. Is that a moral fault? Do they have to pretend? Is there no other prescription? Oh, God, women are in an impossible position!"

"No matter what position it is they'll find it impossible!"

"You make it an intolerable burden for me . . . as if it were a question of what's fair. Oh, this always happens. It's impossible to talk about anything that really matters, anything intimate. You refuse to hear what you don't want to . . . you turn off . . . anything unpleasant, that doesn't fit . . ."

"You're damn right I won't listen!"

"Oh, God, there's no way out," she said and began to cry. "It's always the woman who has to carry so much, pick up the pieces, hold everything together—a man's ego, her own self-respect, the childrens'—soothe, and reassure, and pat everybody's back . . . I sometimes get so *bored* with trying to . . ."

Gerard thought he had stopped listening. He was very angry. He had so full-heartedly expected to find her in all ways mollified, even to acknowledging that she was. But instead, to hear the same old business about not understanding! And what in God's name would be the point of understanding, what possible good could come of it . . . the talking out, this laying things on the table, these confrontations? It was all terrible, all the most ill-advised, misbegotten kind of self-revelation—disgusting! *Insane* to want to say these things, hear them, codify them, verbalize them. Then where were you? With the cruellest words spoken, that couldn't be unspoken, couldn't be forgotten, and no way out . . . and then, afterward, he was the one who had to pick up the pieces, soothe, and reassure.

He had gotten out of bed, and with resentment zigzagging through him top to bottom he turned on Kitty and sneered, "Well, when did you start pretending to be satisfied?" not knowing, once more, that he sneered, that he smirked, or even what he was asking.

"I've *always* pretended to be satisfied," she said in a terrible stagy hiss.

Gerard dressed and left.

The children were in the corridor, just coming to wake them up.

"You know what Mimi told us?" asked Elizabeth.

"What?"

"Mimi says when we go to Mount Etna tomorrow you can see where the Cyclops threw fistfuls of boiling lava after Odysseus. Just when they were hitting the water they got cool, you see, and stiff. So they stand up there like black sand castles, she says. To this very day, and we're going to see them standing there right in the middle of the water . . ."

"I thought Mimi didn't speak English," said the father coldly.

"Annie taught her," said Elizabeth. Annie looked modest but uneasy.

"You're up too early. Mother isn't dressed yet. Give her another half hour," he ordered, and he left them.

He walked through that long morning, heading down the cliffside, then across to the beach of pobbles, along the railroad track, until he came to a station. His memory was having an orgy, and old accusations and indictments that he had not really heard were breaking one upon the other through the surface. Humiliation jockeyed with self-pity. Extravagant scenes formed in his mind, annihilating dialogues, killing answers, and his lips moved. And yet, although Kitty's charge on the face of it was devastating enough, there were layers and layers of mitigating evidence beneath. And Gerard, even at the moment that he was flattened by the blow, knew simultaneously that Kitty didn't mean to say what she said because it wasn't altogether true. Wonderfully insensitive though he was, he knew that by some diabolic need in himself to insist, some litigious need to be relentless, to prove himself right about whatever damn thing it was, he had once again pushed Kitty across the line; that he was in part responsible. This gave him leeway in the denouement.

He sat on a bench in the small station and the time rolled on. A single train came and went. His conclusion that his marriage was finished, that he could not possibly with self-respect continue to live with Kitty, had weakened and given way to the assumption that he would continue, and to a vague, amorphous sense of shame, of failure, that predominated over anger, over everything, and at last he got up and walked back along the track and up the mountainside to Taormina. He was in time for lunch. Elizabeth had fallen and cut her chin. He made a butterfly bandage for it.

Thirteen

THE Winters children had been, as usual, with Mimi when Elizabeth had cut her chin, so that they had to come back to the hotel to wait for their mother or father who were out. But Mimi was very comforting and had lent her handkerchief, and by the time they reached Mimi's rooms, Elizabeth wasn't even crying. In fact Mimi had all three children fascinated by the true story of Cinderella and the glass slipper. Originally it was a French fairy tale, she explained, but not so interesting as the one we know.

"In the French story," said Mimi, "the slippers were made of squirrel fur . . ."

"Well, that's really much more likely!" said Annie.

"Of course," Mimi agreed, "and more comfortable, wouldn't you think?" They would think! they certainly would think!

"Now, listen carefully," Mimi went on. "The French word for squirrel fur is *vair*, which sounded to the English exactly like *verre* . . ."

"Glass!" yelped Annie. "Do you get it? I get it!"

They all got it. By accident, even Virginia Hume got it, because the doors to their rooms were open, and she was just heading toward them when she was startled to hear Mimi's voice speaking English, loud and clear. She had hesitated, backed against the wall of the corridor, and listened, and become indignant as the devil. Her first impulse was to dash in and say something like "Aha!" and her second, upon which she acted, was to scurry off, not to be caught catching.

Virginia Hume, as with most people, found it much easier to be angry than to feel hurt, and as with some people, she had, gradually, through the years, made provision against being hurt by curtailing the number of friends and relations who could close in and do it. These systems of defense are set up without very much conscious intent, it seems, and are faulty. There were places where Virginia was vulnerable and because they were not many, they were probably the more painful. Why had she come to Sicily? Why really had she stepped out of her own tidily arranged daily life, lent herself to the discomforts, not to say tackiness, of a tourist bus if it were not for her deep caring for Mimi? Virginia was a woman who had a great sense of self-possession, at whatever price it was bought, and she rather single-mindedly and with confidence followed Mimi here so that she could guide Mimi by precept and example into the repossession of herself. It did not enter into her understanding that Mimi, in spite of their special affinity, a special tacit tie that bridged time and oceans, did not want to have her misery picked over, nor her cure administered, by this proficient aunt, or by anybody else, for that matter.

All along Virginia had been very skeptical indeed about the language amnesia that was supposed to have befallen Mimi. She restrained comment about it because in case it wasn't real amnesia, then it seemed such a transparent and yet desperate dodge as to touch her with both pity and embarrassment for her. So, while she fiddled with the packing for their departure next day, these familiar doubts were turning over in her mind, and she was assailed now by anger, now pity, now skepticism, and again uncertainty, until finally she was able to reorder her emotions so that, by reserving her pity for Mimi, she could direct her anger against Cass and Alexia, make them acknowledge the disparity between Mimi's having put them all out so and her rather carefree recovery: that disparity at least. To do that she had to track them down. They had gone off to the cathedral. She started in pursuit. But waiting in the little square in front of the cathedral there was a hearse, an outsized Bentley hearse, the presence of which made her uneasy about intruding, but she guessed her brazen relations were in there anyway, so she braced herself and slipped in to see.

It was, as usual, very dark and it took a moment for her eyes to adjust. At the altar the funeral service was in progress with perhaps thirty mourners all in black clothes, and black veiling, little dwarfs beneath the high vaulting from which was suspended a magnificent black wrought-iron lighting fixture looking like the jet rosary of God himself. Alexia and Cass had taken two camp chairs at the rear, thinking, no doubt, that they were inconspicuous. She thought they were not inconspicuous. Alexia had laid out her drawing materials on a third chair and was intent upon copying the rosary design. Cass, leaning with his elbows on his knees in a comfortable sprawl and taking twice as much room, was reading the *Paris Herald Tribune*, without any self-consciousness. Virginia would have found them amusing ordinarily, but she was there with an ax to grind, and slipped into a chair next to Alexia's inks. The chanting up ahead, the responses, the little tinkle of the bell as the soul flew up to heaven, those sounds were nearly lost in the vaulting, and Cass and Alexia gave her a rather hearty welcome, believing evidently their voices did not carry. Virginia thought their voices carried well enough. Abruptly the Mass appeared to be over and as the pallbearers retrieved the casket, Virginia, now feeling too exposed, took off to watch from behind a pillar. The little black procession walked slowly up the aisle, passing Cass and Alexia, who were bent over their several occupations in the most prayerful attitudes.

When the cathedral was emptied Virginia went back to her camp chair, pulling it around a little for her confrontation.

"Listen, you two," she said coolly, "I have something to tell you. Mimi's speaking English."

"Good," Cass said unperturbed. "I knew she had it in her."

"Ach," she said impatiently. "You talk as though it were a problem of constipation. Did *you* know, Alexia, that she was speaking English?"

"Well, I always knew she *could*, Virginia."

"How the hell you have the crust to be so casual about the disappearance of her symptom, I don't know."

"It was *your* symptom actually," said Cass.

"My symptom?"

"He means *you're* the one who doesn't know French, you see," said Alexia.

"Good heavens! You're nothing but a pack of cards!"

"That's why we depend on you, my dear. You're the sane one."

"Sometimes you take me so lightly, Cass. It's cruel."

"Nobody weighs in more with me, you know," he said, rolling his eyes.

Alexia was bent deep over her drawing.

"You make a fool of yourself!" snapped Virginia. "At your advanced age, with your horny innuendoes."

"The older the stag, the harder the horn! But you're right. My time of life," he said expanding grandly, "man's a fool if he chases young virgins. *Never* had a taste for virgins, *you* know. Fact is, looking for a woman my own age. If you were ten years younger!"

"I think they're attractive," said Alexia, squinting into the vaulting.

"Who?" asked Virginia.

"Horny old men."

"So does your sister. Must be in the blood," said the father.

"Mimi? What are you talking about?" Virginia snapped, scenting the track.

"A horny old man," said Alexia, and stared at the altar with a spiritual smile.

"Go *on*," said Virginia, annoyed, and nearly stamped her foot on Alexia's foot.

"For years. He was in her office. An economist from London. Cass knew him when he taught at Oxford. His children are grown up now," said Alexia, and her head recommenced bobbing up and down as she looked from the nave to her drawing pad.

"Keynesian," said Cass. "Once had some interesting things to say about credit mobility. Burnt out."

"Not all burnt out," said Alexia.

"You and your farmers!" Virginia snapped. "When did she tell you?"

"She didn't," said Alexia. "She told Kitty Winters, and then Kitty made enough oblique references to Cass until he *couldn't* ignore them."

"What are you going to do about it?"

"Well, I don't know there is anything to do about it, Virginia," said Alexia reasonably.

Virginia gave an irritated tisk and said, "I knew it must be an affair!"

"Actually," said Alexia, "it seems she wasn't his mistress . . . More a keeper of his conscience. She took the whole family under her wing. When she was in London she was always going to the zoo."

"Don't know whether the whole business wasn't all in her head," said Cass.

"One hasn't a clue what he thought," Alexia agreed.

"And what happened?" Virginia asked.

"Thing is, broke the rules, and in a rather cowardly fashion, one might say!" said Cass in a voice that affected paternal indignation, "if it wasn't all in her head. Got a divorce, on the sly, never told her. Then one day comes around to announce he's going to marry somebody else!"

When Virginia left the cathedral she was more hurt and angry than when she had entered; and it was too bad, as long as she had strayed into a sanctuary, that she couldn't have prayed for a little peace from all these people. Since it was clear enough that Mimi didn't want to confide in her—went to great lengths not to, in fact—and that Cass and Alexia had closed her out, she was bound to feel pretty bad. And since the reasons for her rejection by them lay in their fuzziness, their hesitations and irrational compunctions, their incapacity to take any action whatsoever, she stiffened, tightened her lips, and began to say less and less to herself. She did not even ask herself what ought to be done about Mimi. She did make one attempt to see Kitty, from whom she might have learned a little more about the romance, but Kitty wasn't available.

Fourteen

THE Winters children did not know how lucky they were to have parents who did not shout or swear or take a sock at each other: who did not have scenes. They did not really appreciate the silent tension that took place instead. It was their way to withdraw out of earshot from the awful racket of that silence when it descended, and through the last afternoon and evening of their stay in Taormina they kept to their rooms, packing, writing post cards, playing solitaire, popping off downstairs once in a while for a short spell of Italian TV, but not popping into their parents' room. There was no violence on Italian TV. It was all in the streets.

This silence between their father and mother, the little time they were together, was particularly solemn. However, by evening Gerard had put in a sufficient number of hours to have spent his interest in himself, but not before he had achieved a kind of standoff in his mind in the form of a couple of rhetorical questions: Why would he find himself emasculated by Kitty's implication that he had never really satisfied her? Kitty had never really satisfied him. Why wasn't that a devastating thought? Why wasn't someone devastated by that? He found comfort in this formulation, whether from fatigue or from regaining a sense of balance by having managed an equal distribution of causes and effects.

In fact, for a moment, he altered the balance in his favor. Certainly he would never tell Kitty what Kitty had told him. How can you expect to have lived with someone from youth to death without having been witness to a few unspeakable truths one about the other? And what do you do about it? Well, you don't speak them. Intuitively, you don't speak them, blurt them out. Intimacy could not survive it. He was confident that Kitty could never drive him to blurting out what he knew. But then he saw—once again he was visited by this new insight—that he could drive Kitty to it.

During the meals, the child-tending, the packing, there was a dismal distance observed through which Gerard almost did not even look at Kitty. Once in passing he thought her eyes were red, but he didn't give a damn. By the time they were ready for bed, however, they were throwing out little bridges, exchanging remarks and small courtesies, evidently proceeding from habit on the wayworn return to normal. Unbelievable, he thought. That this devastating eruption should even seem to subside so easily, be so under-recorded, was baffling to him. He was halfway between laughing and weeping, still in balance. And through the night in which he did not believe he could have closed his eyes, he slept so soundly that he didn't know whether or not Kitty had tossed about in proper torment.

Kitty slept, but as to proper torment, she had put in her time. Her revolutions of mind, from remorse to anger and bitterness, from self-pity to compassion, from defensiveness and self-explanation to exhaustion, were not unlike Gerard's turning over of all his known rocks. She felt deeply ashamed of what she had said to Gerard and at the same time she was incensed at how unfair it was that she was made to say it. Just who was holding the strings, who assigning the parts, escaped her. She was made to say: You, Gerard, never satisfied me. But in the first place that was an exaggeration, really not altogether true; and in the second it wasn't an important matter to her, more or less because long ago so much else grew rich and diverting. What enraged her was how righteous, how childish, how insensitive and unreflective a man allowed himself to be about his own sexual performance, particularly as he grew older. So that it wasn't enough for a woman to be an affectionate partner. Absolutely not enough! She had to be terrifically enthusiastic, provide this constant necessary minimum flattery to his self-esteem. And in case her response had actually modulated with time, she had to perform a charade, always pretend. It was not the sexual act itself Kitty protested but the willfulness of a man to let so much hang on it, a willfulness that with age became selfishness, a kind of desperate selfishness. And it was that touch of desperation which kept a woman tender and compliant, and turned her into a victim.

She loved Gerard. But sometimes she was exhausted with

being married. The smothering intimacy had her choking for air, had her burst out with those cruel words, left her grieving for the pain she gave him, gave herself. Of course her eyes had been red.

Next morning there was sufficient distraction for Gerard in getting everybody fed and the luggage down. Then there was the terrific amount of good fellowship as the tour members got themselves collected again, and there was little Ina back on schedule, holding the reins of her great big bus. She had the reins, but no longer the whip hand. Times had changed, the power had shifted, from when she knew everything, when they, her charges, were at her mercy. Now they were the insiders, and with their own center of command. The doctor was their center of command. The colonel came over to Winters while the luggage was being stowed, gave him a manly clap on the shoulder, said "Perfectly marvelous weather!" and shook his hand.

"Thank you," said Gerard.

"He'll never be able to keep it up," said Cass prophetically, at his elbow.

"Keep what up?" asked the colonel.

"The fine weather!"

"Who?"

But Ina was prancing about, clicking her fingers for them to board the bus, and the passengers moved down the aisle choosing their seats with an upperclassman bravado very superior to their original craven obedience. No more clustering neatly in pairs toward the center front, they were all over the rear, seat-straddling, seat-swapping, and even the little band of teachers from Bergamo had broken out of their circle to the extent of chatting with Signor and

Signora Piazza and the elderly trio from Milan. Cass and Kitty Winters sat together, Virginia Hume was by herself at the back, and Gerard, coming in last, took the empty front seat alone. It was known fondly as the death seat because it allowed one the experience, particularly when the bus was going downhill, of believing that the driver was not watching and had lost all control.

Gerard sat impassively as the driver backed and filled to get the bus through, out of, and down from, Taormina, a dinosaur out of a mouse maze. The morning sun had the sea twinkling blindingly and the bus ran north along the shore and along the railroad track Gerard had followed the morning before. He marveled at what a ridiculous bastard he had been yesterday, so much sound and fury. Today he was a dead weight, a residue, all but insensate. Just a single idea oppressed him, that through the time ahead there were nothing but endless roads, endless tracks. The bus slowed so that they could see the Cyclops' fistfuls of lava that he'd flung after Odysseus, still standing rigid where they froze when they hit the water. Gerard heard Elizabeth's exclamation, Annie's exegesis. He chewed the wing of his glasses without which he could distinguish nothing at the distance of the sea.

Some miles on to the lowest slopes of Etna they came to a massive bed of ugly lava and the bus stopped, and they all had to get out and walk on it and pick it up and examine it. Lava requires an imaginative, high-spirited mood to invest it with any interest whatsoever, which the children had. Their pockets bulged with lava. Allowed once more to proceed, Gerard returned to his place in the bus, opened discreetly a new fiasco of chianti, poured the wine into the one glass he'd bought for the purpose, and put the bottle back under his seat. No passing back, no sharing; he wasn't clubby today.

The road wound through citrus groves, through little towns with their streets and sidewalks paved with lava, and gradually upward where the small fields rolled and vineyards were terraced, yellow and bare under the winter sun. Gerard drank his wine and chewed his glasses wing, and Alexia came by and slipped into the seat next to him. He had forgotten about Alexia, almost entirely. Very mildly stirred, he handed her his nearly empty glass. She finished it off, and he went about refilling it.

"Did you prefer to die alone?" she asked, referring to the death seat. He made a sign of dismissal as if to say he didn't care who died with him.

Whether he could have taken Alexia straight, without the wine, he doubted. But through the wine, and through the sudden change in the morning light, he could look at her chamois-colored cheeks, the fresh green-painted eyelids, the gold rings in the ears, but not the nose—he could run his eyes about her face without visibly shivering or flinching at this woman whom he had so lately imagined within his province.

"Do you know what?" she asked.

"What?"

"Mimi began to speak English yesterday."

"Is that so?" he asked, pretending an interest in Mimi he certainly didn't feel.

"And today, Virginia's stopped. However, in her case it's the only language she knows."

"You mean Virginia isn't talking to anybody?" He smiled

in spite of himself, moving cheek muscles for the first time in a long time. Alexia shrugged her shoulders in honor of the inanity of things.

"Poor Virginia. She never married, never had children of her own," she said not very sadly, "and she has always had something of a proprietary feeling about Mimi. I seemed too intractable for her, but she felt she understood Mimi. However," she said with another shrug, "Mimi, I guess, didn't want to be understood. When she recovered her English, she certainly didn't say a word in it to Virginia."

"Poor Virginia never had children because she couldn't find 'someone who didn't please her, who wasn't her type?' " Gerard asked, needling, sounding cynical and unsympathetic, and content enough to let Alexia see him in the independent state of ill nature.

"Alas for poor Virginia, I think she found at least two," Alexia answered, unneedled, in her usual impassive way, her gaze drifting. "For years she was the mistress of an Englishman who was somebody at Barclay's Bank in New York. It was a daring role to play in those days, but she was very principled about her independence. As the family legend has it, the situation could have been regularized, he would have gotten a divorce, but she wouldn't allow it. Eventually he was transferred to Cairo or someplace and that was that. But he took care of her money and she came out with a boodle. After that there was an actor . . . I don't know . . . Anyway it had a quick run and she came out with nothing. It makes it all perfectly clear, I think, why she would be liable to think in romantic terms about love affairs, because by extension it lends an importance otherwise missing to the defiant style of her own younger years."

She turned toward Gerard with a look of the mildest concern and added, "You know, if you are ruffled about my extrapolating from Swann's observation that afternoon when we walked up to the Castello, I want to say that I felt quite free *because* you and Kitty are so alike, are of a kind. I never make *generalizations* in which the particulars aren't excused from conforming."

Gerard, who had not been at all ruffled about Swann, was now extremely ruffled by Alexia's somewhat mocking assumptions in regard to his marital felicity. She seemed to be sure enough about the felicity but laid its achievement to a certain necessary dull-wittedness on the part of the principals. He was tempted to say, "I notice you don't put your marriage on the block," but he said instead, "We seem to be heading into a storm."

It had become very dark. There were even flurries whipped by a wind. The change from those sunny groves and slopes was something to wonder at, and the children's voices could be heard doing that. Little Vicky turned up to tell her father it was snowing. She wriggled past Alexia's knees and onto his lap, the better to see.

"We must have driven into a cloud," said Alexia.

"A cloud!" cried Victoria. "Do you mean I'm inside a cloud?"

Their bus passed one car and then another, little Fiats, pulled over to the side, with people piling the old snow from the banks into the luggage racks on top. It was bewildering. After a while it seemed that countless cars were coming down the mountain with snow in their luggage racks.

"Well," said Alexia to Vicky. "I don't think there's snow any place else in Sicily and so it must be very exciting for people to drive up here for a look at it. And then probably they want to bring some back to show their friends. That must be the explanation."

"But it'll be all melted!" said Vicky, laughing out of her New England knowledge.

"It doesn't seem too well thought out," Alexia agreed, laughing with her.

"No," said Gerard in a tone of rebuke, "the snow is used for refrigeration." Against his intention he was amused, especially as a cavalcade of these cars was coming down now, almost bumper to bumper, slowing and skidding on the freezing surface of the road. Something like a blizzard seemed to be whirling around them, reducing visibility and the bus was grinding and lumbering up the weaving road, or weaving even where the road did not. They stalled and started again and again while their cloud continued to produce its blizzard. After a long half hour during which everybody stopped talking to watch, they arrived in front of a great sprawling lodge and were let out.

Gerard trudged, hunched, ducking his head, through the fine dry drifts with Vicky in his arms and thought things looked a lot like Watertown, Maine, in January, when it was in the path of a Canadian northeaster. It seemed clear to him that they ought to turn right around and head down while they could, not that he cared what the hell they did. And no anxiety creased the brows of their leaders. Ina ushered them into the lodge in her chirpy and perfunctory manner, and the driver's face was its customary soccer-pool blank.

In the main hall of the lodge there were several dozen young holiday-makers, short, smiling Sicilians in costumes roughly *après ski*, evidently not anxious either about the weather. A lot of them, in this thick and sporty clothing, were bouncing to rock music from a jukebox, while others were gathered near an immense stone fireplace with half a tree burning in it. For the newly arrived tour members who believed they had come at last to the seat of Titans locked in a mountain fastness, the hall was no mead hall and was frankly a disappointment. Nothing festooned it, no bloody trophies, no captured flags, no white piles of human bones, not even carpets or draperies or sofas. Only the hearth was a giant's hearth. Instead of bones, there were a lot of kitchen chairs pushed out of the way of the dancers, and there was the little jukebox, whose colored lights swirled and blinked, but it must also be said spirits were not dampened by the plain ambiance; they rose in fact to the rafters. Then all at once, at some mysterious signal, every-body dropped his dancing partner, abandoned the fire, and each for himself beetled out of the hall to the doors of the dining room. It was the second sitting.

The dinner was not a disappointment. Piles of hot pasta, carafes of wine are not by nature disappointing. A thick plank table covered with white linen was set aside for the tour group in a corner of the dining room, away from the snow-blind windows, and the bus driver announced that it was Ina's birthday, and somebody ordered champagne, and then somebody else. Possibly it was always Ina's birth-day on Mount Etna, a caterer's happy thought, since it was the last communal meal of the tour, but the members of this tour at least did not need the champagne to stimulate their sentimental feelings. Signor Piazza had already announced in formal English that he would assume with pleasure the duties of the host country, duties, he said, which had been urged upon him by the teachers from Bergamo, the Fondini family from Milano, and especially Signora Piazza, and that in the name of the Italian people and with confidence of a unanimous approval he had reserved the places of honor for the doctor and the doctor's wife and their three beautiful daughters. There had been great applause. The three beautiful daughters turned round-eyed and flushed with pleasure as with glistening braces, slipping glasses, and a missing front tooth, they were discovered to be, after all, swans. Kitty, who had walked in with Cass, and Gerard, who had been about to sit down next to the colonel, found themselves stranded at the top of the table, cheek by jowl, their bristles brushing. The children were on either side. Every face among the party was turned toward them, nodding, smiling, confident. These people had created the Winters in seven days, had deposited in them the best sense of their own selves, had rewarded them with success and happiness, and they were confident that Gerard would stand up now and look at what they had done and say that it was good. Gerard knew it. He thought it was a particularly cockeyed misassessment, and in his head rang the voice of Cass on their first day out: "A fiasco, eh, doctor? Name of the game!"

He was about to respond willy-nilly but was haply forestalled by the announcement of Ina's birthday and the diversion of champagne, which was not, at first, very good champagne. After that, Kitty said, "You'll have to say something. You'll have to thank them."

"What'll I say?"

"Say you're proud to be an American," said Annie.

"Yes, and the father of such beautiful girls," said Kitty, lending herself fulsomely to this farce, not appearing to be seared by the irony of it at all.

"And a man who owes everything to his wife," Gerard added without, he thought, showing a trace of his own searing; because immediately and once again he felt swelling through him a tide of rage against Kitty, a rage that was impotent, that branded him impotent, that made his hands tremble and his temples pound. Or it was the champagne. Without her advice and consent, he ordered the next round, at God knows how many lira, and when it was poured he rose to his feet. Everybody quieted at once and looked up to him, and he said, in a false, hearty, wine-soaked voice, to an audience whose discriminating ear was by now dead, that he would like to offer a toast in the name of the grateful people of Paris, Baden-Baden, Manchester (England), Brussels, New York, Washington, and Boston, a toast to their gracious hosts and kind friends, the Italian-speaking people, and he drank his glass to the bottom.

Somehow this was found to be immensely satisfying. The hands-across-the-sea motif was admired for its brevity and its modesty, one had to suppose, and as Cass said later, it was ecologically sound, old fellow, not a thought wasted. Everybody was now subsiding to attend to the remainder of their meal when all at once and very grandly, Mimi arose from the bottom of the table like Venus from the sea, and her face suffused with passion instead of wisdom, and her

hands spread wide in preparation for the bestowal of a
blessing, she glided in all her angelic magnitude toward
Kitty and Gerard. They both found themselves rising in
awe as she approached them. Taking first Kitty's hand and
then Gerard's between her own, she held them steady on,
searched the eyes of one and then the other, and at last
proclaimed in a throaty English, "You are my ideal."

She had put Gerard into a trance, but Kitty broke the
spell. She murmured "Oh, Mimi," got their hands free,
gave her a little hug and walked, chatting with her, back to
her place, making it all appear as though this sort of human
behavior was normal. She then returned to her own seat
next to Gerard, to whom she sent not a look or a word,
as though this sort of human behavior was normal. Blear-
witted with drink, and with a lost sense of time, he proceeded through the meal to its conclusion. Word passed
that the trip to the craters was canceled because the roads
up were closed, and that they would be leaving directly
for Catania. Nobody except the children seemed to mind
missing the craters—not, God knew, Gerard.

Back in the bus Gerard took the death seat again, this
time unvisited. He watched the driver bounce in his seat
as he revved up his vehicle, while the strong windshield
wipers slapped back and forth to clear the width of the
window so that there was an unobstructed sense of the rage
of this crazy storm. Ina sat cross-legged on her perch by the
door, her expression complacent, as it usually was. Gerard
crossed his own legs, bracing himself with the ball of his
left foot, crossed his arms, shrugged his shoulders, chewed
the inside of his cheek, and otherwise prepared for disaster.
He did not have long to wait, and it was very satisfying.

Only a few hundred yards down the road the first curve to be negotiated was not negotiated. The bus plowed head-long through the guard railing to a smash. Of course, it was everybody's good luck that the mountain was on the other side of the railing instead of the valley. But there was an extended hullabaloo before gratitude became the dominant theme.

Fifteen

THE toll of this disaster, modest by Sicilian standards, was two concussions, one broken arm, one cut lip, and a few minor bruises. The concussions, logically and fairly, felled the driver and Ina, who were both made unconscious and had eventually to be carried moaning back up to the lodge on litters. It was Frau Fassbender of the bursitis who was the single tour member to be seriously wounded—a break in the humerus—and probably the best prepared, since she had never succumbed to the seduction of their group, all along feeling that she was being the victim of this and that ineptitude. The cut lip was little Vicky's and for a few glorious minutes, with the blood spilling out and widely smeared by several fingers, she looked quite ghastly, as if it were the reign of Herod again, and somebody had put the sword to her. Kitty mopped her up.

Immediately two professionals rose to the occasion. Winters, of course, to attend to the individual predicament, and Cass, for whom disasters were a stock in trade. The front door of the bus had been buried in the snow bank, while the body of the bus hung a bit high in the air for the emergency exit to offer easy egress. But since the doctor's stethoscope was in his luggage underneath there was a certain urgency to get at it so that he could be seen to prove with his instrument what he'd already said without it, that Ina and the driver were not dead at all. Frau Fassbender was clearly not dead, repeating "Why should this happen to me?" at intervals in German in a good, strong voice. The emergency door did not work and Cass, with a swing of somebody's tote bag, not only broke the window and cleared the glass, but easily hoisted himself through an aperture appearing to be one half his size. His two daughters and Annie slithered through in swift order, Mimi and Annie with great purpose making their way to the lodge to sound the alarm.

In this emergency the lodge would reveal itself as a kind of hostel from which climbers set out for assorted craters and crevices as well as the summit of Etna herself. It therefore contained not only a supply of litters, but a proper stock of splints and slings and Mercurochrome to treat falls and exposure, and trained people to stand by— but not in January. As a rule, there were no climbers in January because of the storms. So the staff was skeleton, nine young men attached to the kitchen. Nevertheless, to the few stranded day-excursionists still up at the lodge as well as these employees, and including most of the tour members who were not in actual pain, the children in particular, the accident was privately experienced as superb; a wonderful windfall in which fate scooped them up to the top of the world for an heroic, though safe, adventure, cut them off from the predictability of quotidian life until the next day at least. Almost everyone became the player in a grander scene and gave it his all.

Most of the passengers were still trapped in the bus, meanwhile. Virginia Hume stood foresquare in front of the broken bus window but refused to leap through it. Instead she stooped down to read the instructions on the emergency door, which were in three languages and also illustrated, followed them, and it opened. There was a jump and she jumped. Immediately she recovered the use of English in order to bark at Cass: "For God's sake, Peter Pan, all you had to do was lift the latch before you turned the handle!"

Cass and Alexia were attacking the luggage hold, stacking all the suitcases in the snowbank in the search for the doctor's bag. No doubt roused by the sight of their belongings being buried in the blizzard, one by one the passengers hazarded the leap, with Alexia to hand them out, and led by Virginia and Elizabeth, soon made a straggle of refugees, clutching their possessions, heading up the hill, blurring into the storm.

When Gerard had said to himself coolly, "the damn fool will never make the turn," and the damn fool didn't, he was braced and alert for the finest view of the smash. Before his believing eyes, the side of the mountain rushed at the bus head on, and in that split second he saw the driver's skull whack the window and the whole of Ina's tiny self flung against the dashboard. The racket of the collision was followed by a few moments of consecrating silence in a soft white world, and it was that white silence, Gerard thought, which cast its spell, contributing to the illusion that not only the bus trip, but reality itself was suspended, and that he suddenly knew what it was, at a rather advanced age albeit, to land at the bottom of a well or in the land of Oz. It was a mood that prevailed through the ensuing hour or so while he examined the probable extent of damage to life and limb and while the land of Oz became the land of Dr Zhivago, the movie, not the book.

The bus had come to rest on a tilt, so that one row of windows became a wide screen and offered him a very close view of Alexia rhythmically heaving and stowing against a bank of snow. It was she who provided the Russian motif in her greatcoat and boots and with the magnificent addition of a Cossack's hat made of some kind of dark brown fur. Gerard was captivated by the Cossack's hat collecting snow above the fair brow. By the pitch of the windows she seemed, once again, magnified, and extraordinarily clear so that he even saw the pores of her skin. He walked back and forth along the sight of this hat, the brow, the great green eyelids, and the pores, between the two unconscious patients in the front, and the wailing Frau Fassbender in the rear, to whom he gave double the attention he would normally have forced from himself, and with a stop at Vicky, whose mother held a snow pack against the swollen lip. Kitty barely registered on his conscious mind. It erased her. She might have been in Siberia.

And then all at once down through this Russian snow, or down these Russian steppes, he noticed a sledge coming, at a sort of chugging pace, and crouched at the front in her red coat and red cheeks, with her noble head held high, and with the expression of a proud maniac, was Mimi, triumphant with litters and litter bearers. Dr. Zhivago, late of the Slough of Despond, found himself lifted into the thin air of some celestial comedy. He breathed deep.

Kitty took Vicky off and finally the bus emptied of all but the injured who were neatly laid out in the aisle. First Ina and then the driver began coming to and groaning, and Alexia soothed their brows. At the other end, the doctor wrapped Frau Fassbender's arm against her side for support while she howled. It was very Russian, that howling— wolves. There followed the transfer to the litters and the assignments to the litter carriers, and finally Gerard, who was Bezukhov now, brought up the rear with his two Russian countesses.

It was a question whether without Cass this small calamity could have been turned into a kind of folk festival, whether, for instance, the tour members would not more probably have sunk in spirit, and sat listless on their luggage by the fire waiting to be taken care of, whether one of them would even have thought to find another half tree to throw on it. But for Cass, it was another jungle, a realm where he was king, and he thought of things like infrastructure and commandeering as naturally as doctors in the old Hollywood days used to think of hot water and plenty of it. No more had he strode through the doors of the lodge and said "Un telefono, subito!" than the young steward who was chief of the skeleton staff sniffed his aura, bobbed his knees, ordered wood for the fire and whiskey all around against exposure, and led the way. The two litters with Ina and the driver had been carried to a small anteroom, which Cass, swinging through, said would not do. Where, he asked, were the director's private quarters? The steward, very fine about the wood and the whiskey, showed a nervous reluctance to give away this information, but with a glance at Cass, whose expression was an imperious blank, he yielded. The apartment, with two rooms and a small bath, delighted Cass and he congratulated the steward warmly on the charm of its appointments. Flattery and fear struggled on the face of the steward. Cass commandeered the rooms. In the one which was a sitting room, there was a desk with a telephone below a wall hung with framed and autographed pictures of skiing champions gripping their poles. There was a worn Turkey carpet on the floor and an electric fire. Cass plugged in the fire and settled down to a battle with the telephone.

When Gerard and his two Russian countesses came along not ten minutes behind, the nurses were already making up the beds of the patients. Frau Fassbender had been put in a chair by the window. She was still wailing and Mimi slipped to her side and murmured German to her. Frau Fassbender listened to Mimi and stopped fussing in order to correct her German. Her coat had been eased off but they had to cut her blouse. Gerard thought she probably had a break in the humerus.

"A little crunchiness, a little crepitus there," he said to Mimi. Mimi translated. "No need to do more than immobilize the arm against her side," he said, and proceeded to do it with yards of gauze and ace bandaging. Frau Fassbender said that was not the way they did it in Germany, that they would certainly have a hospital and a plaster cast and a sling. Gerard gave her some codeine to take every four hours.

And then Cass called out, "Mimi? Get the gnädige Frau the ge-hell out of here, will you?" and Mimi led her off to the dormitory wing.

"Alexia?" he called next. "Run round and see how Signor Piazza is managing with those kitchen boys and the generator, d'you mind?" Alexia spoke Italian.

Between attempts to make a connection to Catania, or anywhere else, in a rather breezy manner, with a finger pointing, he waved his arm about, and by this magic brought into being a happy and efficient little army in which everybody was a general and important, and all the generals trundled off to stoke furnaces, check boilers, make beds—there were two dormitories with thirty unmade beds in each—tend the wounded, cook the pasta; it all seemed to happen within a matter of minutes and with wonderful enthusiasm. The next room was converted to a dispensary, and Kitty and Virginia were converted to nurses.

"What a leader of men!" said Kitty with relish, by which she actually meant women. She was talking across their patients to Virginia, who could not have looked more skeptical. Gerard bent over first Ina and then the driver, nudging each of them in turn, and they groaned miserably. He was returning to earth from the Russian orbit. Ina worried him. She had vomited. He straightened up, and frowned into space and then frowned at Kitty for being flighty, and then walked into the next room to see Cass. This frown was not lost on Kitty. It refired her indignation.

"Really, Cass is marvelous!" Kitty repeated with even more relish. "He thinks of everything! This is what professionalism ought to be."

"Nonsense," said Virginia dryly. "He hasn't left the telephone."

"And everybody in the highest spirits!" Kitty went on indomitably. "It's like the London blitz!"

"Colonel Blimp," said Virginia.

"I say, Virginia?" Cass called from the next room. "Fellow on the line in Catania wants to know how many people there are up here altogether. In particular he wants the passport numbers of the foreign nationals. Can't seem to interest him in anything else."

Virginia, with an exasperated shrug, walked into the next room and asked impatiently, "Is that damn fool going to get anybody up here tonight?"

"Well, y'see, problem of landing a helicopter. No visibility. Easy enough matter in the morning. Roads clear quickly. Like our spring storms, don't you know."

"Well, tell your little friend you can't talk any more now," she said sharply. "Tell him you've got to walk through the ranks and cheer up your troops. You can have a nice chat tomorrow!"

Cass considered her for a moment. Then a great admiring bellow came out of him, and he said in English to his interlocutor, who just possibly did not understand, "My mother says I have to hang up now," and he hung up.

Gerard found himself laughing at the buffoonery. And Kitty, God knows, was laughing, and too eagerly from his point of view, and his anger against her revived once more because she was insisting upon this display of carefree girlishness for his benefit and before Cass and Virginia, a poor performance they must certainly, he felt, find terribly transparent. And tasteless, with Ina lying in there very possibly in trouble.

He wasn't satisfied with Ina's degree of consciousness, was concerned that she might be developing a coma. He went back to the next room and sat on the side of her cot, touched her cheeks, wiped her forehead, talked to her. She groaned for him. How much more human she seemed half dead, he thought, a limp little Flopsy who bit her nails, with thin arms and knobby elbows and knees and almost no breasts.

They were still horsing around in the next room and he went in and cleared out all the clowns—Cass, Kitty, Virginia, everybody out! He was going to watch things down here, he said. He was going to watch things down here *by himself*. They were perfectly glad to go.

Sixteen

BEFORE the accident, during that wild farewell lunch with the poor champagne, when Mimi had risen out of her seat to issue her passionate declaration to the Winters, Virginia Hume had felt an ominous shiver. She was somehow unprepared for the sight of such a large field of coral roses on her green Italian knit dress, and then for those blazing eyes in such a coral-colored face. Ordinarily Virginia had a great skepticism about blazing eyes. But the implication in regard to Mimi, that she might be mad in English as well as in French, was a wrenching revelation to her. The hurt she had felt on being left out of her confidence dissolved in pity. Virginia took an unsentimental view of other people, but she had always allowed Mimi to range in a kind of preserve protected from her normal insight, her critical appraisal, since the day she was born; fortunately in New York. A premature infant, they had hovered over her, fed her with an eyedropper. She, Virginia, was there and fed her with the eyedropper, a sack of pinched skin and tiny bones who looked like the fetus of some smaller animal. What a cruelly warped portent of the size of Mimi to come that was! If Alexia had gone in for blazing eyes it would have been quite another matter, although she suspected Alexia's eyes would be the last eyes to blaze.

Virginia's heart was taken by an ache that was not usual with it, but event so swiftly followed event—the storm, the smash-up, the struggle to climb back up the hill, the organizing of the lodge—that the tragic plight of Mimi, whose face bobbed into view simply glowing with joy, became neutralized in the confusion. If Virginia had not been confused she would have lined Cass and Alexia up against the wall and shot them down: because, as she saw it, they permitted, they tolerated Mimi's insanity; they sided with it, were in collusion. Alexia, with whom she found herself alone counting out blankets in a large cedar closet giving off from the hall between the dormitories, would therefore have been the first to be shot. Shooting Alexia would have diverted Virginia from asking what she herself proposed to do for Mimi, or to Mimi.

But Alexia, who piled without counting, said, "Do you know what Kitty's done? They have a summer place on the Cape and she's asked Mimi for July. Mimi's beside herself, quite out of her mind."

"She certainly is," said Virginia tartly, still counting.

"Oh, she'll be all right *now*, Virginia. She's got the Winters for ballast. She'll be back on an even keel. You'll see."

"She's not *sane*, Alexia."

"Well, that puts her with the ninety-nine per cent. She'll be all right. You'll see," she repeated confidently. "After all, in town with grandpapa she leads a quite profitable life.

And everybody when his heart is broken is entitled to fall apart. That's *appropriate* behavior, I would have thought. The only peculiar thing about Mimi is that she falls in love with whole families. It's queer to you and it's queer to me, but it works perfectly well for her, and then, of course, when the thing breaks up . . . but here she's found another whole family, wonderfully suited. They're really very difficult to come upon these days—whole families. I think one would have to say, things being what they are, that Mimi's lucky in love." She paused for a moment, and then added, as though it were conclusive, the final nail in the argument, "Look at Proust. He slept all day, and he worked and was up and about all night. He tried to change, but he found he couldn't. So he went to the end of his life sleeping through the day."

Virginia found her mind scattered, so that she had no answer for Alexia. But she was not made unhappy by this. On the contrary, she enjoyed being in the cedar closet, for instance, and sniffed, and wondered if the cedar was from Lebanon. People were coming and going for their blankets as if it were one of the highlights in the show. All their lines were funny presumably, but in Italian; only Alexia could have said. The beds were being assigned by Signora Piazza, the erstwhile restrained and formal Roman matron who was proving to be the most fiercely efficient of the generals, and who was eliciting the most boisterous compliance. The reassuring sound of human laughter was punctuated with the more reassuring sound of pipes clanking and banging, presumably to be followed by a rush of heat into the wing.

Kitty was in charge of sheets in the linen room. The linen room had some old stuffed chairs in it, and when the parceling out was accomplished Alexia and Virginia joined her for a rest period out from under the surveillance of Signora Piazza. Kitty had a bottle of whiskey Cass had slipped her and so they dropped themselves deep and happily into the lumpy upholstery, stretched their legs, and got refortified by nipping, as through time must generations of housemaids have done.

"Alexia tells me you've asked Mimi to visit you next summer," said Virginia to Kitty. "It's made her very happy."

"I hope it'll be all right," Kitty said uneasily. "She's got a rather idealized view of us."

"What she worships, really, is family life. She's only known a poor substitute," said Alexia in a sort of shorthand that took care of all Mimi's bad experiences.

"I only knew a poor substitute myself," said Kitty in a musing tone, and thinking the reference was to childhood. "If I look back it seems I had the full complement of people and events—a house, a mother and a father, a bicycle, a dentist, a high-school graduation—nothing like the loss of your mother, Alexia. But my mother was very . . . shallow, really, always uneasy about her social standing, about not slipping, and my father . . . turned his back, I guess. I loved him . . . but he was elusive. Anyway, aside from a teacher or two, I just didn't run into any people of substance. I yearned to be in a world surrounded by people of substance. I wanted to *assure* myself of them—and so when I was married I had six children! I was only too successful. After a while I began to feel all these people were piled on top of me. From then on I've just been wanting space, looking for space." She laughed at this story she'd told on herself.

"Does Gerard give you space?" asked Alexia.

"Gerard doesn't know what I'm talking about," said Kitty with another affectionate laugh for him.

"I would have said he was a very generous-hearted man, a giver of space," Alexia observed mildly.

"You don't know someone until you've lived with him," said Kitty, who, Virginia thought, was a little annoyed at having candidly revealed herself to be somewhat less than she seemed while leaving her husband to be somewhat more. "And after you've lived with him you begin to understand him much better than he understands himself."

"Nothing could be more irritating, it seems to me," said Alexia in her neutral tone.

"Than what?"

"Than being looked at by somebody who thinks he knows me better than I know myself. Does Gerard do that to you?"

"No, I do that to him," said honest Kitty, flushing.

Virginia looked at Alexia sternly, but Alexia would not be stopped. "Toddy says he doesn't understand me at all. I find that very acute."

"You're a special case, Alexia," said Virginia dryly. She thought Kitty did not deserve to be tripped up this way and lent her sympathy while Kitty set out to retrieve her standing.

"Gerard in open court would swear he didn't understand me, but nonetheless he's absolutely certain he knows what's best for me. He never questions the logic of his position."

"Yes," said Alexia, and after considering Kitty for a moment, turned 180 degrees. "You are right. A man like Gerard would allow everybody else room but not his own wife and children. Everybody else, however, is grateful for his having . . . brushed by them."

"He's very fine," said Kitty quietly. "Mostly I'm grateful too."

"Oh, dear," said Virginia, who made uneasy noises when something too sweet was in the wind.

"You can't make him see it," said Kitty, demonstrating that she understood her husband better than he understood himself, "but he needs space too, and he's taking it in a most characteristic way, by retreating into the past, by reading Homer, Herodotus, the Greek tragedies. That's why we're here. We would have gone to Greece but for the colonels. It's the moral order of the classical world that gives him comfort. Moral bedrock, he now believes, is that the living only have this earth in trust. If people saw themselves as part of the historical continuum, then ethically things would fall into place and, by extension, life would resume progressing. And yet, he had to be dragooned to stand on a vigil or work for a peace candidate. He hasn't the time, really," she added, now siding with him for the moment. "He hasn't the time, running his course between the Mass. General and ancient Greece to stop and listen to what people are asking *now*, to what they are saying *now*."

"We made your beds!" said Annie now, having burst through the linen-room door. "She wouldn't have let you *eat* unless your beds were made!" Straggling in behind her were Mimi and the other children, laughing with diminishing degrees of heartiness over the authoritarian Signora. Vicky, her lip all swollen, was plainly more worried about not eating than about jokes.

"With hospital corners like a real nurse!" Elizabeth said.

"Mimi showed us. From the minute I get home I'm going to change my own linens, okay mama?"

"When you get home you can change everybody's linens," said her mother, and then to Vicky who had landed on her lap, "Oh, I think they would have let me eat *something*. Maybe not dessert. What a silly noodle you are," she said laughing, nuzzling her child.

"Oh, dear," said Virginia to the child, "Do you know which bed is mine? Can you show me mine?" Vicky left the lap with a very satisfying leap and led the way.

The dormitories were strictly a no-frills affair stretching out in four-bed cubicles with no place to put one's luggage, no chair even, and with a dull bulb dangling at either end of the long room leaving virtually no light to see by. Frau Fassbender was in Virginia's cubicle, but sound asleep. There was a Fassbender checker on half-hour rotation, who would, if she woke, call Mimi because Mimi was the only one who knew enough German to do battle with her. But she slept on. Vicky showed Miss Hume the hospital corners and then the w.c.

Throughout the evening Virginia found herself looking out for Mimi's face, and finding it blooming pink and bright. She was pulled this way and that about her; this way, when she was defensive, and she thought a professional diagnosis would certainly prove she was absolutely right about the insanity. But that way, the preferred way, was the idea that if she could only have a few minutes alone with Mimi they might repair the damage between them, might recover their mutual trustworthiness, the old affection she and Mimi always seemed to have. So much did a restoration of warm feelings lure Virginia that she even put in jeopardy her own strictly guarded privacy, and on impulse suggested to Cass that perhaps it would be a good idea if Mimi came back to New York to stay with her; but he said that she'd spoken on the phone to papa before they'd left Taormina, and told him she felt fully recovered and could be expected back at her desk on Monday morning.

"Trouble with you, Virginia," he said, "you fret wrong. You don't worry in a profitable direction. Take England. My God, people'll say. What'll we do, England is going bankrupt! Well, if the English go bankrupt today, they'll still be there tomorrow. They won't disappear. They'll still be getting up to brush their teeth and drink their tea and so will Mimi."

"Oh, for God's sake," Virginia said, but not with her customary force.

Finally she did catch up with Mimi outside the sleeping quarters on the line for the bathroom sink. Virginia was, by this time and after several second winds, exhausted, and would have skipped the teeth and crawled into her bed without changing her clothes, but she had the dangling impulse to say something reuniting and normalizing to Mimi. Her lovely hair loose and brushed for the night, Mimi was already tidily in her ruffled travel robe.

"Did you hear that I'm going to visit the Winters at the Cape in August?" she asked, smiling with pleasure.

"I thought it was July. How awfully nice. In fact I wondered whether you might want to fly into New York and spend a few days . . . You could stay with me."

"No. We have a much better plan. A reunion! Cass—I didn't think he would be, but he's gung ho. And it gives

Alexia one more place to pop off to—not for a whole month, of course. And you like the ocean. I said to Kitty that you taught a summer course through July. That's why we changed to August. I wouldn't want to have done it without you."

✳ ✳
✳ ✳

Seventeen

ALL the festivities went on upstairs without the beloved
doctor. But eleven different missions crossed the dining
room, wove through the steamy kitchen, and down four
unlit steps, and along an unlit corridor to the director's
apartment where Gerard was trying to sulk in his tent
alone. They were well-intentioned gift-bearing visitors, and
solicitous of his patients' welfare, and he received the blankets, the sheets, four bottles of wine, and the supper while
rebuffing the offers of help and the bodily presences. He
liked his tent. He thought some athlete, some winter sports-
man, was spending the years growing old in it. Shabby,
musty, not overclean, its walls were covered with faded
Olympic posters and framed photographs of champions,
the bookshelves stacked with sports manuals, first-aid manuals, health and exercise manuals, and dirty Italian paperbacks, judging by the covers. In the small sitting room,
there was a good-sized cluttered office desk, and a day bed
covered by a heavy tapestry whose color and design were

wearing away in patches. There was an easy chair and, in the corner, an electric phonograph with a stack of old breakable 78 rpms in their paper jackets.

Of the visitors, Cass was notable for coming down three times out of an abundance of good fellowship, Mimi to report on the perfect docility of the Fassbender, who took her next medication and went right back off to sleep, Kitty and Annie with his supper ("How is Ina?" "I don't know." "Well, see you in the morning."), and the colonel's lady on tiptoe. A senior Girl Guide leader and teetotaler, the colonel's lady opened her large pocketbook, pulled out a bottle of wine from the dining-hall stock, and said soberly, "There's a time and place for everything," and was off.

By eleven all the building echoes quieted and Gerard was left to himself. He tended his patients and would have nursed his own wounds of the soul, but his mind wandered, and he idled about his little quarters, attentive, overstimulated; sifted slowly through the covers of the paperbacks with their good and vulgar invitation to good and vulgar sex, and was frustrated by the Italian language. In time the idling brought him to the record player, and flipping through the records, he came upon an American label, which to his great amusement read *Fred Astaire, A Fine Romance*. On the other side was *Fred Astaire, Cheek to Cheek*. He got *A Fine Romance* going very low and quiet so that he would be sure to hear them if they woke in the next room. The lyrics spilled from his mind, after waiting there thirty or forty years, ". . . You're just as hard to land as the Île de France, I haven't got a chance, This is a fine romance," and he crooned along with a rising pleasure that had no particular memory attached to it. He heard footsteps just in the nick of time to lift the arm from the record, in time to say "shit," but he wasn't caught.

"I have never slept in a dormitory," said Alexia, in a tone that suggested she would not break this rule.

"Come in and close the door," Gerard almost ordered, almost losing his breath while the next event began to follow as the night the day, and Alexia materialized once more out of the unreality of the most intense of his desires. Gerard had been expectant and listening keenly for sounds beyond the sounds of his patients in the next room, so that now when he saw phantom and flesh dovetail with such artistry, he experienced the dovetailing as the greatest surprise and at the same time as the least of surprises. Now he was released from being sole captain of this ship, and he relinquished his hold and allowed himself to be borne along by exigencies, by a momentum composed of intentions only one of which was his intention. There was no time allowed for navigating around reefs.

"Look at this. Look what I've discovered," he said in a normal voice, but he felt his flesh tingle. "This will amuse you." And again he got *A Fine Romance* going, very low and quiet.

At the first bars of the song, Alexia's composed expression broke with recognition. She raised her arms to be danced with, and there was no interval before he was holding her, swaying in the smallest fox trot, to a rising humming through his skull and cheekbones, a humming that began as they sang into each other's ears, she remembering mostly the tune, he remembering all the words. There was an unmeasurable interval before they were lying on the day bed. And then more uncountable time during which

Gerard traveled the arc to a crescendo he had never reached before in his life.

When he had regained his hearing, and regained his sight one eye at a time, he found himself propped on an elbow looking down into the tranquil face of an unfamiliar Alexia. It was as though some unknown girl had strayed beneath him. He dropped his head down to bring the blood back into it, resting it on her breastbone, and when he looked at her again with his good eye there was still some new cast to her face that was mildly perplexing to him. Was it possible, he wondered from out of his euphoria, that he had only seen her constrained and unappeased and that this was the look of release? He decided to take this flattering view. She looked more beautiful than ever, and with her hair undone much too young, uncomfortably young—sixteen—in the dim light and with his glasses on the desk across the room.

He watched her scan his face bemusedly. She didn't seem to have the least need to say a word. Once in a while she drew her finger desultorily around his eyes, along his nose, poked his jowls, traced the creases; the little things pinioned lovers do, confined as they are to one position. With gravity against him, he thought vaguely, his flesh must hang from his face, he must look a hundred, and he hid the face in the hollow by her neck.

After an immense length of time filled, he thought, with an erotic silence, Alexia whispered into his ear, "Would you like to know what Proust's biographer says about him?"

Gerard could only laugh. He rose once more on his elbow to get some air and to shake his head.

"If you read Painter, he says Proust discovered that all our desires are fulfilled on condition they do not bring the happiness we expected from them."

Gerard was taken aback. He was taken aback to hear such an observation at the very moment when all clinical evidence was to the contrary, and narrowing his eyes he examined her face for signs of disappointment. He didn't find them. It seemed to him, on the contrary, that her face had come alive. He said, "I think it is better to read Irving Berlin. He says I'm in heaven and I seem to find the happiness I seek when we're dancing cheek to cheek."

"Over the short haul, some nice coincidence like this. But not over the long haul. Proust is right over the long haul," she said, and relapsed into silence, lying there thinking about Proust, evidently, while Gerard eased himself along side her and was quiet too. Notwithstanding the unmistakable intimacy of their situation he remained diffident about intruding into her meanings. He supposed he was given to understand that it was not a question of landing her like the *Ile de France*, like Cary Grant, that the irony of this fine romance was much more avant garde.

Breaking the silence some time later he said he was going to look in on Ina, and although the light was low he found himself shy about getting up and pulling his trousers on. The driver was coming along, but with a terrible headache waking him. Gerard thought it was safe enough to give him something for it and get him back to sleep. Ina, on the other hand, would be a long watch. He opened her eyelids, he shook her by the shoulder and was able to arouse a protest, he checked her pulse, watched her breathing, looked at the time to mark it down, and was lost in confusion. Two forty-five. "I think there was a lot of wine," he said out loud to himself, as if it were the most significant of her vital signs, and then at the thought that he was ready to return to the next room, his heart took another leap, knocked against his lungs, and he had to draw in his breath audibly.

In the next room Alexia lay calmly on her back, naked as a bluejay, but otherwise unlike a bluejay, and said, "Put the record on again."

He stared down at her before he put the record on again.

Ina was holding her own at three forty-five. By then Alexia had become famished, she said, and they had some cheese, bread, and wine on their day bed, and he, who had previously such firm objections to eating anything in bed, even breakfast in bed, now took the opposite view. The crumbs were all over his chest and stomach and he brushed them off and brushed her off. "After all, I think we're a couple of hot tomatoes," he said needing, evidently, to exhaust the words of *A Fine Romance*.

"Do you know what I was wondering? I was wondering whether Kitty was sleeping with Cass?"

"Why would she do that?" he asked, dumbfounded.

"Well, I looked for them and I couldn't find them. She wasn't in her appointed bed."

"My God, Alexia, it's altogether out of her character. And she's much older than you are. You forget how long she's been *in* character. It's just not the sort of thing she . . . besides, sex is something that isn't a compelling drive for her."

"But suppose it were a compelling drive in Cass, she might . . . be very nice about it."

Alexia looked at him in a noncommital way, carefully

noncommital, he thought. He wondered whether she associated her own behavior with that sort of generosity. In fact he was always wondering about her association with whatever she was talking about, whether she was speaking as participant or observer. Her suggestion in regard to Kitty however was not credible.

"It's too farfetched," he said after ruminating, playing the changes on it, and then he added almost wistfully, "It would be nice if it came out even."

"Well, you'll never know," she said casually. "Or at any rate in my view it's one of those truths that . . . loses something in the telling. It doesn't travel well." She was smiling but he was frowning.

"The other day," he said, "we were having an argument, Kitty and I, about some friends of ours, a couple we know —who would leave whom—and she said adamantly that there were fifty reasons why a woman would leave a man and sex was the fiftieth."

"Forty-eighth or fiftieth," said Alexia.

He was nonplused once more. It was inexplicable to him that Alexia would say such a thing and mean it, and he thought she did mean it. Out of his ranging experience of, now, two women, it seemed to him that sex might even be Alexia's special field of interest. Evidently it was not hard for her to detect the disbelief in his face.

"I mean I would not move any pieces on the board for sex." She seemed confident he would find that a clarifying remark.

"I can't help being curious about what your marriage is like," he said after he decided that it was clarifying, that she would not be swept off her feet for more than a few hours.

"Oh, very different from yours. We don't *cleave*," she said with a trace of distaste.

"I thought you said the other day you were always home with the children."

"I am given to overstatement. I'm *often* home with the children. In any event, I don't cleave to Toddy. He needs a lot of space. He's never home. But in the best sense I'm his springboard. We're very different. He's got immense energy, and I'm somewhat languid. I drift. And he's very ambitious politically. Watergate is going to clear a lot of bad guys out of his way. I see his nose quivering, I see him pawing the ground . . ." she laughed contentedly at the thought of this ambitious horse, her husband.

"Do you love him?"

"Oh, yes. Do you love Kitty?"

He hesitated, and then smiling, he kissed her pretty nose and murmured "Mmm-hmmm," the amused and contented and domestic sound of affirmation that his wife and children would have recognized at once. The amusement was particularly apt since he thought it was bizarre under the circumstances to say yes without at least equivocating. But he was not inclined to tell his troubles to Alexia—hers wasn't that kind of invitation—and the troubles themselves, at least for the present, seem to have been wiped out, seem to have "vanished like a gambler's lucky streak," in the words of the philosopher, I. Berlin.

"Cleaving is going to be the death of marriage," Alexia said philosophically. "Everybody needs space."

"Does Toddy have . . . other women?"

Alexia wriggled her way up to a sitting position and considered him seriously. "You mistake me, Gerard. You think that when one says space one means sex. That's very male. Everybody needs a vacation, but that doesn't mean everybody always goes to Yellowstone National Park. In fact, it is particularly unwise to choose sex when one lives in a place like Washington and one's husband has an eye even possibly on the Senate. I would never choose it. It's a cliché that Washington is a small town, all gossip. And Caesar's wife must be above suspicion."

Having delivered herself of this explanation, she lay back on the bed again.

Gerard looked down with raised brows upon this naked woman and she added, "Caesar's wife *when in Rome*."

They dosed off for a little while but Gerard was aware to his marrow of time spinning to its end, and he kept pulling himself up out of a deep sleep in order to see her lying on his arm at peace, with her eyes closed. There was no green paint on her eyes. When she woke he said, "I want to ask you an impertinent question. Did you forget the green paint or did I eat it?"

"I want to ask *you* an impertinent question. Have you ever slept with another woman, besides Kitty and me?"

"No."

"Well, have you ever gone to Yellowstone National Park?"

"Yes, one summer we . . ."

"Well, there you are!"

He felt a tide of sanity rise up in him in protest, and for the last time in this marathon night the old warrior called on a surge of lust to engulf it, to engulf Alexia. The sleep that followed was exactly like the sleep of the just. She waked him with the gentlest touches.

"Gerard," she said. "Do you know what I think?"

Rolling his head from one side to the other, smiling away at her, he said, "Don't think."

"I think I hear somebody."

In a shot he was out of bed and halfway into his clothes when she asked, "Do you suppose you have a shower?"

"A shower?"

"Oh, I think it's Ina. I think I recognize her particular groan."

"There isn't a shower."

"Well, then, at this point in time I think I will depart your cuckoo's nest and find one."

"Where will you say you were?"

"In bed. And if that isn't enough I will develop additional information, as John Dean is in the habit of saying when the facts are found to be insufficient for his purposes.

Eighteen

THE lodge was rattled and shaken awake by the sounds of total war. People clutched the sides of their strange cots and buried their heads in their pillows, and almost everybody testified later that his first thought was volcano. The Americans, however, had the patriotic idea that their president had decided to save Sicily by his preferred method of wiping it out. The Americans were closer to the mark because it was a helicopter that made the ghastly racket as it landed in the lodge parking lot. Virginia Hume, who had gone to bed with all her things on, grabbed her coat and bolted through the corridors, and was joined by one person after another pulling clothing together. They were making for the veranda.

Once out on the veranda these various people were brought to a standstill. In a split second they took in and dismissed the now quiet helicopter, which was a small disfigurement in the snow, and had come to rest at the corner of the left eye. Ahead of them through the clear cold air was half the sun risen from the rim of the Ionian Sea. Down and across an immense apron of land it was still night; on the lower slopes, in the valleys, along the shore it was really still night.

The sight was so exalting, such a gift of heaven, and for which nobody was at all prepared, that people of the most irreligious temperament were made reverent long enough to watch the sun clear the sea and rise several inches up into the sky. Even Frau Fassbender, whom Mimi had led out wrapped in a blanket, was struck dumb and stayed dumb for a considerable period. The Winters children, their coats over their nightgowns, hung over the railing, all six legs sturdy, all the bare feet dancing in and out of their fuzzy red and blue slippers, but as Virginia noted, their tongues were still. Virginia herself felt she was in danger of being purged, blessed, forgiven, or whatever, and put up her defenses. When those gathered on the veranda resumed their talk and social interchange, the communal spirit took off again, rising to another feverish pitch. People turned to congratulate each other as if they were chosen, as if it were Easter Sunday, even making the mistake of congratulating Virginia. With a roll of her knuckles and a weak smile of acknowledgment, she shook off her fellow celebrants and headed down the steps and through the snow to join Kitty at the helicopter.

The steward, the kitchen boys, Signor Piazza, and above all Cass were having a loud Italian argument with the somber and very official looking men with sun glasses from the helicopter. Cass was in another of his elements. He was by turns gleeful and sly. He had passed the word to Kitty that the chopper fellows were insisting upon the passport numbers of the foreign nationals before making another move, and this was causing his sides to split, and his arm to out-gesticulate the Sicilians proper. Since it was a Red Cross chopper, he said, it was a point of honor that the casualties come first. He would force them to their knees.

Kitty, already trim in her navy-blue stockings, was radiant with approval. "He's magnificent! He knocks me flat!" she said to Virginia while her eyes never left Cass. "We stayed up half the night talking. Vicky was restless because of her lip and I didn't want to keep anybody up, so I brought her out by the fire, and in a minute Cass had discovered a cache of summer porch chairs—he really is some kind of divining rod—and with a lot of blankets we were all very comfortable."

"Oh, he's absolutely marvelous about chairs. Nobody can touch him about chairs," said Virginia, and decided she would try for a bath while people were still absorbed by Cass and other natural wonders. She gave Kitty a wave and had just reached the top of the stairs again when she heard a great booming tenor and turned around to see Cass striding off from the group, waving his arms as if to conduct the sunrise, and singing "And the dawn comes up like thunder out of China-ah! cross the baaay" at the top of his lungs. He was in fine voice.

A familiar robe was hanging over the bath stall.

"*There* you are, Alexia," said Virginia. "Everybody was wondering where the devil you could be. Didn't you hear the commotion?"

"I had the bath running," said Alexia from her side of the partition.

"Well, there was the most God awful noise. They sent a Red Cross helicopter up and it's sitting right outside by the front porch. And I must say you missed an absolutely rosy-fingered dawn . . . But I just don't see how you can have failed to hear that helicopter. Didn't you feel the earth move?"

"Was that what it was? A helicopter? I don't believe it," Alexia answered in a mildly marveling voice.

"It's a circus down there, and your father is flapping about like an overwrought seal. And what's more, he's burst into song.

"Cass?"

"On the Road to Mandalay, with gestures."

"Ah, he used to sing that when we were children. Nobody can do it better, not the gestures."

By the time Virginia herself had bathed and put her things together and was ready for some coffee, a brawl with the functionaries from Catania had been averted and a compromise was in effect in the dining room. Cass was passing papers amicably to the officials across a table by the door. Evidently he was singing under his breath. At the sight of Virginia he kindly raised his voice, and pointing to her he sang ". . . there's a Burma girl a-wai-ting, and I know she *waits for me*" loudly. Just beyond Cass, in the middle of the dining room, with tour members milling about them carrying coffee cups and pieces of bread and jam like a lot of mad hatters, were the driver and Ina on their cots. Tables had been pushed aside and they were exhibited in their faulty condition, on cots, on litters—with the most primitive absence of delicacy—before the world. Virginia found this extraordinary.

"My God! What have you got here? Bodies? What is this, Lourdes? Is this the Ganges? Are they going to be burned?"

"Virginia, my dear, these gentlemen would like to see your passport," said Cass.

"Well, it really is a kind of miracle," said Mimi in a reasonable and placatory voice. She was standing back with Alexia and took the broadside of her aunt's outrage.

"Ina will recover, it seems," Alexia explained. "She was in a crisis all through the night, but she came through wonderfully."

"She says the doctor saved her life," said Mimi. "She said he sat by her side the whole night. He never left her side."

"You don't get doctors like that any more," said Alexia.

Virginia surveyed first Ina, who was in voluble if tearful converse with Signora Piazza, and then the driver, who appeared dazed, but not more than usual. "Where *is* the miracle doctor?" she wondered too loudly.

"Yes, where is the miracle doctor!" Signora Piazza fairly cried out. "He has saved Ina's life! She swears it before God!"

The miracle doctor, in all innocence, strolled through the kitchen door carrying a suitcase, and with a coat flung over one shoulder, and Virginia thought he was yodeling, but he was singing. She heard him clearly, as he passed her, singing a song from her girlhood, "Heaven, I'm in heaven, and my heart beats so that I can hardly . . ." and she muttered, "For God's sake, what's going on with all this singing?" He didn't look to her at all like a man who'd lost a night's sleep. She watched him while he was brought to a halt by one after another tour member needing to offer a few more words of praise. Since he was about to leave on the helicopter with his patients, everybody thought it essential to shake his hand, but they would see him if not at the hotel in Catania that night, certainly at the airport for whatever flight to Rome would finally be secured. She found it a rather attractive trait in him that he never shuffled, never showed any impatience, although he was endlessly stymied in his intentions. It occurred to her suddenly that he was surviving what she suspected was only the penultimate encore of these orgiastic expressions of group solidarity by a rather comical inattention: that he really was impervious to so much adulation, he simply didn't take it in, and she found his modesty, his balance, very much to his credit. He remained in the best of spirits. Annie stood poised, not wiggling, a pace beside her father, her hands behind her back, her chin up, following the conversations, proud, confident, composed, almost, for the moment, the woman she would become.

"Her father's daughter," said Virginia to, as it happened, her mother.

Kitty was watching the performance, very pensive. "Annie?" she said, musing. "She's her own woman. When her turn comes, she'll break his heart too." She was quiet a moment and then she continued with a wry smile, "He's the best of men . . . He has an unbending integrity, and he can't change. Sometimes I think it's a cruel and inauspicious moment in history for the best of men."

"Would you like to have his integrity bent?"

For the first time, Virginia succeeded in nettling Kitty. Friendly Kitty shot an unfriendly look at her, squared her jaw, and said evenly, "A little."

Virginia drew a small breath of achievement and with a pat to Kitty's shoulder, forgave her for being insulted, became the friendly one, and led her to their breakfast. Alexia and Mimi joined them.

"Well, Cass is going with Gerard," Mimi announced with

a laugh. "Signora Piazza said she thought one of us should volunteer to go along to interpret, and Alexia volunteered Cass."

"I don't like Frau Fassbender, I don't like Ina, I don't like the driver, and I don't like helicopters; four reasons," Alexia said in excuse for herself.

"That's what I've got to do!" said Mimi, reminded of another of her self-imposed duties. "Bundle up the Fassbender, get her moving." And she was off again.

"Mimi is strikingly sane this morning, isn't she? Even the fire in her eyes is gone," Virginia felt impelled in honesty to say. "It's simply unaccountable," she felt impelled to add.

"Why don't you let grandpapa's 'change of air' account for it?" Alexia asked.

This was not worth an answer and did not get one from Virginia. Kitty, on the other hand, said, "What she means is a change of place—and, if one is in luck, a fortuitous change of people. New people can act as a catalyst sometimes. So that what happens, I think, is that one is able to make a small . . . correction . . . in the way one goes about life, and achieve a better equilibrium. I'm only talking about a very modest shift, of course, and it isn't the new people who shift you. They are just the spring that releases the possibility . . ." She was speaking modestly against the implications that she and her family had restored Mimi.

But Virginia could let neither the modesty nor, in particular, the psychologizing go without some comment.

"You just said a few minutes ago when you were lamenting your husband's fine character that people don't change."

"I said Gerard won't change," said Kitty, her voice tightened.

"Well, as you have confessed, you know him better than he knows himself," said Alexia, "but I think Gerard, as well as the next person, is entitled to be thought capable of making a small shift."

Kitty flushed. "Do you notice a shift in yourself, Alexia?"

"No, you're right. Quite clearly there are those who are exempt. I am exempt, and Virginia . . . Virginia would be aghast . . . and we would all be aghast for you, Virginia."

"Fate's cruel, Kitty," said Cass, who had swung into the empty chair by her side. "Be a damn sight happier flying off with you than with your husband, I can tell you." And he put his arm around her shoulders.

"They're picking at me, these harpies of yours," said Kitty, her good humor altogether restored by the arms of Cass, as it seemed. "They're picking at my weaknesses."

"No, we're picking at her strengths," said Alexia.

Virginia thought weaknesses, but forebore to say so. Kitty was on her nerves. Instead she said, courteously pointing the finger away from Kitty and onto circumstances, "It's eleven. We ought to be landing in Rome just about now. The last twenty-four hours have been a strain."

"Best hours in the lot, *my* opinion," said Cass, looking affronted, pouting, and raising his brows to Kitty for support.

"Yes, best," she agreed, smiling at him.

"Yes, best," repeated Alexia.

"No question," said Gerard, who appeared in time to offer his opinion to the panel.

Nineteen

Iᴛ was a rosy winter dusk in Rome on the day following the rescue from Mount Etna. Gerard was being hustled along the crowded sidewalks toward the Colosseum, being constantly bumped over because he wasn't watching his step, because his eyes were searching the shop windows for his own reflection. He expected some indignant citizen might heave him into the street, although with the evening traffic there was no room for a body. When he caught his reflection in the glass he caught the face of a superbly accomplished man, a man who didn't have to explain a goddamn thing, not to anybody, not to himself.

"I'm not going to explain anything," he said, half aloud, and the sound of his own words conjured in his mind a picture of Kitty, with her chin up, saying, "I will never explain a phone bill again." He wondered if there could be a trade off here, and the thought struck him as very funny.

They would never have gotten to Rome at all if it weren't

for Kitty. All the extremely complicated business of money, of finding another flight back to Boston, finding them rooms in Rome on New Year's Eve, all the things that took his experience, his special competence, Kitty handled. It wasn't difficult, she said. He had slept right through. The last thing he remembered of yesterday was returning from the hospital with Cass to the hotel in Catania, finding his family just arrived and installed, and telling Kitty he had to close his eyes for twenty minutes.

When he got to the Colosseum, he scanned it for the particularly lousy restaurant Cass had gone to last summer, and inside he was lucky enough to get a table by the window, with a perfect bead on the corner Cass must have watched. He ordered a Campari-soda. Certainly a lot of people were rounding that corner, a lot of men, but he hadn't made allowances for the one factor that would queer the survey: the weather. It was the middle of winter, the last day of the year. Everybody was wearing overcoats and gloves, or his hands were in his pockets against the cold. The fascinating phenomenon Cass had observed turned out to be as seasonal as soft-shell crabs. Thwarted in their pursuit of the behavioral sciences, his thoughts abandoned the Roman street corner, and settled in ancient Greece; such a traveler is the mind.

"No man can call his life happy until he's dead" is what one Greek after another said, and every time Gerard ran into it, his back would go up, he would, in metaphor now, pat all his parts, and then he would demur. Suppose, he had thought, he were cut down tomorrow by an unexpected stroke of fate, he would be prepared in fairness, in justice, to testify that until that stroke, his life had been (speaking, of course, broadly) a happy life. Afterward, other people might say, "There lies Gerard H. Winters; he lost his shirt." In the minds of other people he might in the end only have made his mark by the nature of the calamity that hit him when he was fifty-three. But for himself, he hoped he was as ready as a man can be for the unexpected and that in the event he would have the magnanimity to acknowledge the happiness that came before it. This was the happiness of a man who pretends he had asked very little, and pretends he has got a great deal, and ties the whole thing together by seeing duty as peremptory and absolute. It would not cross the mind of such a man that fate's unexpected stroke would be magnificent; would be nirvana, a night in Xanadu, would be a boon and prize that sent him soaring to an Olympian peak it was never in the cards that he should soar to.

"Too bad we didn't get to the peak," Elizabeth had said that morning, the child who had to be reminded that she sometimes could not see the doughnut for the hole.

"There are more peaks," he said firmly, and at once became dizzy at the thought of another ascent. However, he carried even into the state of euphoria his habit of measuring, counting, evaluating, and hedging against the future. There would probably be no sequels to the episode of Etna. Still, it was possible, nonetheless, that they might all turn up at the Cape next summer, even Alexia, and if her predilection *coincided* with his again, he might manage, albeit by the most extravagant departure from his expectable behavior, to be summoned back to Boston for twenty-four hours. But thinking now about how was thinking about birds in the bush. It was much more gratifying to think of the bird he'd had in the hand, to reconstruct and revel in those hours with the bird, minute by minute; no cages, absolutely no wire, and what a test of his prowess, what an overachiever! He put down a second Campari-soda oblivious of the world around him, helpless with admiration for himself.

It might be seen that he had to fall back upon himself because whatever else was unclear about Alexia, she was not in love, was not even infatuated, and had no intention of proceeding in some orderly fashion toward a future clandestine assignation. Somewhat quizzically she returned his few subtle, private glances before their parting as though they were giant winks and whoever winked like that was crazy. But orderly proceedings were in the very nature of Gerard and he was able to put Alexia's short memory to one side with surprising ease for the purpose of directing a flattering appraisal of himself.

He had become his own mock hero by having made an unprecedented departure (he flinched quite properly before the word transcend), from the safety of his lifelong exemplary behavior. He had laid siege not only to Alexia but to his own rectitude, he had ventured himself, albeit on the strong tide of beckoning circumstances and because he was closer to blind drunk than courageous; and the proof of the pudding was that here he sat two days later and still with no regrets, no sense of guilt. And he thought, take it all in all Kitty would be pretty damn well surprised at him. It was a shame he couldn't tell her.

Meanwhile, the irony, he saw clearly enough now, was that it was left to him to reaffirm the proposition about his happy life. In spite of the heaven he glimpsed and kept singing about, he hoped he would still say, still have the magnanimity to say, that before this particular supernal stroke his life had been happy, and that unless disaster came around the corner, he would be able to resume saying it was happy; maybe not immediately. Somebody else might say that to experience such a high pitch of pleasure was ineluctably to throw everything that went before in the most vapid and flat relief, unacceptably flat. Before it was too late, while he was still as alert and virile as a boy, between attacks of arthritis, the dentist, headaches, he would grow a beard, this other fellow, buy a black turtleneck jersey, and move into a garden apartment from where all the next moves of this sort seem to be made.

Gerard had a noncommital sigh for the other fellow. For himself he thought he was just by nature an incorporator, and that he would just have to find room in his happy life for a short experience of romantic bliss, and meanwhile there always remained the possibility of disaster, and he looked out at the corner to see whether it was coming around. But John was coming around. It was five, and Kitty and the children were to meet him here at five.

"Where's mother?" he asked, as John took a seat.

"She's gone with the girls someplace Cass talked about. She says she'll meet us back at the hotel in time for dinner."

Gerard's first thought was that Cass had Kitty sitting in some other café window counting something else.

"You know, I meant to tell you," said John, "I met a guy in my class, went to grad school in economics, and he's here on a Ford Foundation grant with the Club of Rome now, and I asked him whether he'd ever heard of Henri Cassagrande. Well, Jesus, didn't he ever!"

"What did he say?"

"Nothing. Just he was something. I thought he was out of his tree, myself," John said, meaning Cass. "My God, the whole lot of them, I thought they'd lost their keeper."

How awful are the young, how awful are the young, his father hummed under his breath, but said aloud in a voice philosophical and false, "One of the things traveling lets you do is have the companionship of people a little stranger than you might want to take on in your daily life. It can be very refreshing. Look at mother," he said hypocritically. "She's coming home positively on the wings of song! After a week with Cass in the sixteenth century! But Cass in Boston, Cass for dinner with the Levinsons, ogling Eleanor, telling jungle stories . . . Now does mother want all that?" Fortunately John wasn't listening so he didn't answer. Gerard thought she certainly did want all that.

"I won't even mention Mimi," said John, following his own line of thought. "Just take Alexia." He paused, and with a hard and uncompromising look at his father, to whom he had issued this order, he handed up his indictment. "Do you know that all she reads is Proust? That's absolutely all she reads. In French. She took me up to her room once to show me. Her mother gave them to her. There were these three little beaten-up leather volumes that looked like prayer books. You remember how grandma used to make me have a prayer book when we were in Watertown and she made us go to church? Three prayer books. I'm not kidding."

"Do you know why she reads Proust?" his father asked, reaching into his breast pocket for the answer he had written down. " 'Because he discovered that all our desires are fulfilled on condition they do not bring the happiness we expected from them.' "

"If she read something else she might pick up another idea. Then she'd have two," said the son, whose responses were not entirely satisfactory to his father, who anyway smiled at the snotty kid.

They retreated to their own thoughts. After a while Gerard kindly asked his son whether a few days by himself in Rome had helped him think out his problems with Lisl. Immediately all the brassiness left John. His shoulders dropped, and he presented himself as defeated.

"I think if I held out long enough, I could force her . . . It's just for her sake. I just don't like to see her in a situation where she's demeaned."

"You may be fooling yourself. You may be afraid to see yourself demeaned . . . living with her without having her name on the dotted line, you know—not having been able to get it all nailed down."

"I thought you were the great apostle of marriage," John said, annoyed. This had been made very clear in the fall when his sister Kate came home with the good idea that she could save on room and board by living with a guy at Tufts.

"I am, but I don't believe . . ." said his father hesitantly, "I don't believe one ought to *force* somebody to accept the logic of one's position. I think, John, you've got to choose. Either you find a girl who agrees with you innately about this, and fall in love with her. Or you take Lisl with her right to independence, her defiance, as part of the deal . . . as part of the givens if you're going to make some long-range thing together. After all, a case could be made that it's her nice irrepressibility makes her worth the candle. I think I'd make that case."

John became pensive and turned his chair a little as a signal that he'd had enough advice. His father, the apostle of marriage, began to wonder, on his part, what centripetal force was left, besides sex, to make two people like Lisl and John hang on over the long stretch. Not children, evidently. Sex wasn't dependable. It was too ephemeral, and what one wanted was staying power, continuity. Maybe, he thought, some updated dynastic view where family tradition and history and family things could have some leverage: where the things held the center together, and you held on to the things. Then you would ride an arc that came out of the past and thrust into the future. Every Greek hero knew who his grandfather was and wanted to be buried by his grandchildren. Solon said the man who had the happiest life was the man who died in battle and was buried by his grandchildren. Well, skip the battle, the point is, he thought, that the family should rest on something more noble than my lust. Just so long as I'm buried by my grandchildren . . . nothing about whether my wife is pleasant, whether she gets her doctorate or runs for the United States Senate; nothing about whether I slept with a goddess or, for that matter, whether she slept with an economist.

"I don't see where I'm going to get the grandchildren if some of you don't give in and get married." he said out loud.

"What?" asked John, who had plainly been miles off.

"I said there are fifty reasons why marriages don't last and sex is the fiftieth."

John decided he had had enough of his father and drifted off.

When he was gone the father returned straight away to the consolation of the Greek point of view, which was the next moment sidetracked by a rush of sensuality that for a long while took up all the space there was, and he was late getting back to Kitty and the children.